Inanimate Things

Edited by Stephen Rhoades

Cover Art © 2024 by Ruth Anna Evans
All Works Edited by Stephen Rhoades

E-Book Edition ISBN: 979-8-9894535-3-5
Paperback Edition ISBN: 979-8-9894535-4-2
Hardback Edition ISBN: 979-8-9894535-5-9

Published by:
Burial Books LLC
4000 Eagle Point Corporate Drive
Birmingham, AL 35242
www.burialbooks.com

Contents

The Maul

by Chelsea Pumpkins

To all students, faculty, and staff of Popolac University:

It is with heavy hearts that we return to our campus community after the tragic events at the women's rugby game last Saturday. We are all grieving the untimely loss of nine of our own students and the critical injury of six more, whom we wish a full and fast recovery. We offer our sincerest condolences to the Norwich Capitals for their immeasurable losses on the pitch as well.

Our elite sports programs here at Popolac unite us in the spirit of teamwork, dedication, and pride. To experience such a catastrophe at a match where students, players, and families join to compete and celebrate is truly horrific.

Please join us for a candlelight vigil at 7 PM Wednesday, October 25th. Additionally, we are offering and encouraging individual and group trauma counseling sessions. You can register for free on our health services portal. You'll also find many support resources there.

If you or someone you know is in crisis, help is available 24/7 at 800-273-8255.

Now, more than ever, we need to take care of each other.

Stay strong, Giants.

Sincerely,

Madeline Clarke

President

***

I'd braced myself since the call from the agency on Saturday night—this would be my highest-profile assignment yet. I hadn't worked a large-scale tragedy before, but I needed to start somewhere. My director always said, "Confidence comes with experience."

I chewed my nails down to the tender edges of their beds, and my fingertips throbbed as I folded my clothes. My brain banged incessantly against the back of my eyes, presumably from my clenched jaw. Packing for the trip to Popolac was no problem, but charging my emotional batteries for the oncoming barrage had been a fool's errand. The only sleep I'd gotten was on the short plane ride here, and I had Klonopin to thank for that.

At least the university was accommodating. Hospitable even. They set me up in a private office with its own bathroom and tiny kitchenette. I had just finished pouring my first cup of coffee when a curt knock struck the frame of my open office door. I took a sip, burning my tongue, before answering.

"Yes." I suppressed a cough. "Come on in."

Grayson Young—women's varsity rugby coach—peered into the office before stepping in. He was shorter than I anticipated, from what I'd seen on YouTube. Specks of gray dotted the black scruff on his cheeks, and heavy bags sagged low beneath his sunglasses. His clothes were mismatched and wrinkled, but he smelled clean.

I hadn't expected him to be my first walk-in.

"Hi, uh, I'm here for the..." He shifted his hands in his hoodie pocket. "Is this the..."

"I'm Celena." I waved my hand, signaling him to enter. "The trauma counselor. Coach Young, right?"

"Gray is fine," he said.

"Gray, then. Nice to meet you. Please," I gestured to the sofa, "make yourself comfortable. Can I get you something to drink?"

He shook his head, lips pinched, and sat down. He flexed all ten fingers and pressed his palms against the top of his knees as if kneading dough. I grabbed my legal pad and pen from my desk and sat in the pleather armchair across from him.

"I'm glad you're here, Gray. Why don't you tell me why you came today?"

He inhaled deeply. "Well, to start, the athletic director mandated it. I need you to clear me before I can get back to my team... What's left of it."

His flexed hands curled into fists.

"I don't know. Maybe we should just cancel the whole program. Maybe I should leave Popolac. Find another school. Maybe another sport. Fuck." He pressed his fingers to his eyelids as if trying to plug holes in a dam.

I felt the urge to wrap him in my arms, rock him while he cried. They said this part of counseling would get easier with time, but that tide of sympathy has yet to recede. Warning bells rang in my mind: *Countertransference.*

I cleared my throat.

"Let's back up," I said. "Tell me about the game on Saturday—the incident. A chronological rundown, as you remember it."

"It's hard to say. It was so fast and so...grotesque. One moment it was a typical rugby match, and then the field was littered with bodies.

"I guess it started when Joan got tackled. Got dumped right on her head. You could hear that thud across the pitch, and I just knew. You can't mess around with head injuries."

I hummed in agreement, waiting for him to continue.

"Joan took a knee, and the ref blew his whistle. I went out to check on her. I try to keep it casual when my girls get hurt. Lot of times they're in shock, or confused, and I don't want my reaction to make them panic. So I asked her real calmly 'What's going on, Joan?'. And she answered something weird, kinda funny." He huffed, almost laughed. "Something like, 'I'm good, Coach. I was seeing stars, but the sky is clear now,' and she waved her hands in the air like she was wiping a window. I knew then she was done for the day. Joan's a funny one, but this had concussion written...well, in the stars, I guess."

I smiled, pleased he was opening up.

"So, I helped her off the field and caught up with our captain—we call her Brix, but her full name is—was—Brianna Rigsby. Brix ran up to me, nervous because Joan is our best back, and we were down by three points. We needed to win to make the playoffs. Losing Joan at that point was a big blow. When I looked at the bench, I didn't have a lot of options. I chose Chrissy to sub in."

He stopped then, lost in a stare through time. Trapped in a memory.

"Chrissy subbed in," I reiterated.

"Yes, Chrissy." He nodded. "Christina Rogers. She isn't—wasn't—our best player, not even close. But she *was* one of our best teammates. She knew how to pick us all up during a rough match. If you needed a pep talk, you went to Chrissy."

"She sounds special."

"Very special. They all are." His voice hitched. "Were."

"So, what happened to Chrissy?" I asked.

"Chrissy was the first one in."

"In?"

"The maul. The...skirmish, the tower."

"I'm sorry," I interrupted. "Pardon my ignorance, but I'm really not familiar with rugby."

"Right, sure. No problem. We had just won possession of the ball and were making our way down the pitch, just passing and running. Chrissy caught the ball at some point, and she ran into contact with the Capitals."

"She was tackled?" I asked.

"No, she was still standing, with the ball, but she was bound up with players from the other team, which makes it a maul. Chrissy had her back to them and wrestled to keep possession of the ball until one of our own could bail her out."

"Got it," I said.

"Brix got there first. She tried to rip the ball out of the snake den of arms, to free Chrissy and move the play, but there wasn't much use at that point. Chrissy was swallowed. The Capitals' arms wrapped tightly around Chrissy, from back to front, pinning the ball against her chest."

I tried to keep my eyes on Gray while scratching notes on my pad. Not that it really mattered; he was telling his story to the dead air above my left shoulder.

He continued, his voice speeding up. "Brix grappled at the arms on the ball. Any time she could pry one hand off, two more leeched on. Brix got frantic—it wasn't like her.

"She screeched and clawed at them, drawing bloody scratches down their forearms. I could see the gashes from the sidelines and thought the ref would stop play, call a penalty. But before he could, more players swarmed the maul.

"Both sides had to be at least three rows deep, the players swimming over each other and grabbing for the ball. I could hear the slap of each new body running full speed into the fray, and Brix and Chrissy were pressed together in the middle of it, facing each other, cheeks turning blue. The ball was a linchpin between them.

"Next thing I knew, the two of them seemed to float into the air." He glanced toward me, but I maintained an earnest look to urge him on. "They were...*rising*. The maul was pushing them up, somehow.

"The players climbed up one another, pulling themselves up by fistfuls of jersey and hair. Ripping it out of each other's scalps. Anything to get higher, closer to the ball. The grunts and yells all blended into one mangled growl. It was...inhuman."

"Wow," I whispered.

Gray shook his head. "I watched these smart, carefree women transform into something rabid, out of control. One jabbed her fingers into another's eyes and up her nose, gripping her face like a...bowling ball. They dug their cleats into teammates, tearing flesh right off the bone.

"This maul kept growing taller, and no one stopped it. I should have done something," he said.

"It's natural to freeze up during an emergency, Gray. It's not your—"

He held his hand up. I felt bashful for interrupting and made a mental note to take a beat next time.

"The rest of the players on the pitch charged into the maul. I don't understand it. They became *more* brutal, lost complete sense of the game, as if their *goal* was bloodshed. There was bashing, slashing, cracking, and the ground beneath them turned redder and redder. Within a minute or so, the maul—the tower—lost stability. Both teams swayed, and the rest of us held our breath. The women toppled to the ground.

"People screamed from the stands and sidelines. Some ran toward the fallen players, and others rushed out of the stadium. It was chaos. I raced onto the field."

He winced.

"Gray?"

"I just... I have this really distinct memory of the turf sloshing under my shoes. The field was soggy with blood. I don't think I'll ever forget that feeling."

He rubbed his forehead. "Before I even got close, I could tell some of these girls had to be dead. The way their necks were bent. The slaughterhouse smell of it all..."

My hand clapped over my mouth, holding back the acid rising in my throat.

"It's a coach's worst nightmare, a player dying in a game. Reality is, it happens once in a while, and every game day I pray it won't be me. Won't be *us*. I'm responsible for these young women.

"I see their parents at our matches, and I shoulder the obligation for keeping their daughters safe. Losing one is unbearable. But a whole team..."

He squeezed his warm brown eyes shut. Tears spilled over their rims and streamed down his pale cheeks. I debated against pushing him further, afraid to shove him over the edge of grief.

"Coach — Gray, sorry. What about Chrissy?"

"Look, I feel responsible for all of them being killed, even just being injured. I'm never going to get over that. But I *handpicked* Chrissy. I scanned our bench players, looked her in the eyes, and sent her right into that insanity. I put her in a position she wasn't used to, wasn't ready for. I chose her to die." Gray inhaled a trembling breath.

"When I made it to Chrissy, her torso was flattened, like she'd been leveled by a steamroller. All her ribs must have folded in on themselves. Her face was blue, and her eyes were still open, dripping blood from their inner corners. Blood spilled from her ears, too, into a pool under her head." He buried his face in his palms, his elbows balanced on shaky knees.

I reached my hand to his shoulder. "None of their deaths are your fault. Not even Chrissy's. There's nothing you could have done to stop it. It was completely unpredictable, a 'once in a million years' kind of accident…"

"Then I must be one hell of an unlucky bastard."

I clicked my pen and laid it down, silently questioning how I'd write this session up for the athletic director. Gray answered for me.

"You know? I think I'm done here," he said.

"Okay, no problem. We can schedule a follow-up if you'd like."

"No, I'm done. With rugby, Popolac—all of it."

He didn't leave me a chance to respond. He stood, bowed his head toward me, and marched out of my office. I broke down as soon as his footsteps fell out of earshot.

***

The chatter of women's voices ricocheted down the hall as I arranged folding chairs into a semi-circle for the rugby team's group session. I placed a couple new boxes of tissues on the coffee table and opened the lid of the donut box. These were critical details, but they're also a calming distraction, a grounding routine. I couldn't deny I was particularly anxious about this meeting. I was brushing dust from the back of a chair when they arrived at my door.

"Hi there, come on in," I said.

A girl with brown skin and a bandage over one eye rode through the threshold in a wheelchair, pushed from behind by a white brunette. Three more players sulked into the office behind them. While they all played what looked like a game of musical chairs, I read the back of their matching team t-shirts:

Ruck Maul

Screw Maul

We're Just Here to Have a Ball

Go Giants!

Might as well have been a foreign language to me.

"Welcome, Lady Giants, help yourself to—"

A harsh scoff interrupted me. The brunette's eyes flashed across the circle to the sound's originator and then back to me. "Sorry, we can't stand when people call us *Lady* Giants. What is a lady giant anyway? Does she wear humongous high heels? Giants are just giants."

"My mistake. Let's start over. I'm Celena Hays, the trauma counselor. You are?"

"I'm Joan."

"Nice to meet you, Joan." I eyed the team. "I'm counting five of you. Should we wait for any other girls—sorry, ladies," I cleared my throat, "players?" My armpits dampened with nervous sweat. I know they're grown—technically, they're women—but sitting across from me, wounded and vulnerable, they seemed so young.

"Uhh, nope. There are no others...anymore," Joan said. She looked beaten down, haggard.

"Right. I'm sorry." *Strike two.* "I have coffee, water, donuts—they're all yours. Get comfortable. Oh!" I jumped up to grab a stack of napkins off the kitchenette counter. As I turned back, I noticed a thick trail of staples snaking down the back of one of their heads, blonde hair shaved away around the crusty scab of the seam. The girl in the wheelchair caught me staring. I averted my eyes to the clock over the doorway, pretending to check the time.

Joan grabbed a chocolate-covered donut with rainbow sprinkles and chomped into it as I made my way back. I sat, breathed a cleansing sigh, and started a timer for the session.

"I'm glad you're all here today. It goes without saying you've been through an extremely traumatic event. This session is a place for you to process that without judgment or expectations. Do you have any questions?"

Nine eyes stared back, accompanied by crooked scowls on bruised faces. The smacking sound of Joan licking frosting off her fingers broke the silence.

"Oookay," I continued. "So, I have Joan here, would the rest of you introduce yourselves?" I rested my hands atop my pad so my jittering knees wouldn't rattle the pages.

They went around the circle. Molly was in the wheelchair, then Joan, Shana (her arm in a sling), Syd was the blonde with the head wound, and finally Olivia, who, like Joan, didn't appear to have any physical injuries.

When I offered them the floor, each of them stared at their hands, waiting for another to crack first. I can do silence, but we didn't have unlimited time. After a few awkward minutes, I pushed.

"From what I've gathered, there was a maul in the game that went horribly wrong." I glanced at Joan—she seemed to be the spokesperson.

"Don't look at me. I was concussed. I saw some crazy shit, but I feel like I wasn't really there, ya know? Like, it's not my story to tell."

"Of course it's your story to tell," I said. "You're a part of this team."

Joan sucked on her bottom lip and nodded, accepting the invitation. "Well, I don't remember too much about getting tackled, but my memory slips back when the crowd in the bleachers started murmuring, all at the same time. I was already dizzy, so it was really disorienting. Coach Tad ran over to Coach Young, and they looked serious, talking quiet and fast. I got off the bench for a better view, and when I got to the sideline, Brix and Chrissy had to be, like, almost as tall as the uprights. That's where I start doubting if it was real, or if my brain was playing tricks on me."

"It was real," Shana chimed in. "They were, like, a human tower. But they weren't working together, not like they were boosting each other up. They were *hurting* each other." Her voice was strained.

"It's okay, Shana," I said, pushing a tissue box toward her.

"You don't get it, Miss," she replied between sniffles. "We're more than teammates. We're best friends, roommates—"

"Girlfriends," Syd added in a low murmur, her gaze cemented to the floor. Olivia gently rubbed her shoulder and nodded.

"We would never hurt each other," Shana finished her sentence. "It's like they were under a spell, possessed, hypnotized...I don't know. But they weren't themselves."

"So. It was real, Joan," I said. "Does it help to know others saw it too?"

"Maybe, sure," Joan said. "But there was more." She cracked the tab on a can of Sprite and took a gulp. "The ball, stuck between Brix and Chrissy... It was glowing. I swear. It had, like, a halo of golden light around it, shining bright, pressed between their chests. Reminded me of those old paintings of Jesus, with his heart surrounded by rays of light. No one else seemed to notice, and I even yelled to Coach, 'You see that? The ball? Does the ball look weird to you?'. But he didn't answer. Figured it was probably just my head—you know, auras and everything."

She had all the ladies' full attention now.

"I dunno, Joan," Syd said. "I think maybe it was your concussion."

Joan continued. "It got weirder, still. The girls' faces in the maul...they changed. They got darker, like when you dial the contrast up too high on a photo and all the shadowy parts of your face turn black, and the details disappear. And their eyes." Joan closed her own. "Their eyes blared red, like little fireballs." She opened them again.

"I mean, it *could* have been blood, but I really don't think it was. I was standing next to Olivia, all the way on the sidelines, and I watched hers change right in front of me."

Goosebumps bristled down my arms.

"W-what?" Olivia asked.

"Yeah, something changed in you, Liv. You, like, straightened up, somehow stood taller, looked stronger. Like you were hulking out. And your eyes flashed red for an instant."

Olivia stared at Joan, tears rolling down her face.

"You clenched your fists and started *toward* the maul. With blood already spraying everywhere and girls wobbling in the air. Why would you run into that?"

Olivia shook her head. Speechless.

"Coach and Tad grabbed your arms to stop you," Joan continued, "and you screamed and thrashed against them. Tad had to hold your arms down in a bear hug, and you were angry, manic. You bit into his bicep—ugh, it was so gross." Joan shook her hands, trying to shed the memory from her skin. "And I swear, Liv, your entire mouth was black. Your gums, your tongue, even your spit. Pitch black."

"I...I don't remember any of that."

Joan had momentum now. "The pitch was a warzone. Fingernails turned into claws, teeth into fangs. They would do anything to get that ball. Everyone's screams sounded like this demonic roar in my head. The kind of sound that rattles your skull, like metal pans clanging around."

She paused a beat, staring at the miscellany on the table.

"I still see it in my dreams, or nightmares, I guess. My friends turned into monsters, clamoring to get to that golden ball. It always ends the same: dead eyes open on slack-jawed faces. Those tiny little turf beads stuck to their blood-drenched skin. Limbs bent at wrong angles with shards of bone jutting out. The wet gurgles of a choked last breath... I hate going to sleep. I try not to sleep at all. But even when I force myself to stay awake it's all I think about. I can't keep reliving this."

"Oh, Joan," I started, my voice cracking, but she cut me off.

"I can't help but think about where I'd be if I never got a concussion. It should have been me out there, not Chrissy. Maybe we wouldn't have even gotten into a maul. Or maybe I'd be...dead too."

"You are here, Joan, and this is where you're meant to be," I said. I don't know how the same could be said for Chrissy or Brix, but it felt like the right thing to say to Joan.

"My dad tells me I'm lucky, that my concussion saved my life. But I dunno. What if my concussion set it all in motion, ya know?"

"I know what you mean," Molly said. She picked at the edges of the armrest on her wheelchair. "How can we feel lucky when they're all dead? I'm no one special, but somehow I'm alive and they're not. I can't help but wish I went with them."

"You're meant to be here, Molly. Look around at this circle—they're all here for you," I told her. "Don't be afraid to lean on each other."

I wanted to keep them talking while they were on a roll. "Molly, do you want to share what that day was like for you?"

"Okay. I guess," Molly agreed. "I play fullback, the last line of defense, so I stay near our try zone most of the time. This maul was on the other side of the pitch, so I was just keeping an eye on it.

"I knew something was really wrong when I saw Priti kick Rae in the mouth. With her *cleat*. Deliberately! Rae's mouthguard went flying, and a bunch of teeth rained onto the turf. Might have been her whole mouthful, but it was hard to tell because she spewed blood immediately."

I ran my tongue over my teeth, an involuntary reflex, making sure they were still rooted in place. Molly kept on.

"I can't explain why I ran into it—I shouldn't have. I don't even like getting tackled in practice. I just felt pulled to it, maybe like you, Liv. I could swear I even heard my name being called from the center of it all."

"Do you think it was one of your teammates?" I asked, caught up in her story, forgetting my role for a moment.

"No. It wasn't a scream or a call for help. The voice was so calm, I don't even know how I heard it." Molly twirled her thick black hair around her fingers. The more she spoke, the harder she pulled at the strands. "I sometimes wonder if I dreamt it.

"Anyway, I ran full speed down the field and—I'm really not sure I should even be saying this part..."

"It's okay," Joan replied.

I hesitated—there was no legal immunity here—but I let her go on, despite my gut telling me not to.

Molly resumed with a grimace. "I leapt onto my teammates' backs. I...dug my nails into someone's neck—to keep from falling. It was an accident." She looked at her right hand. "And all my nails broke off in her skin."

My palms felt clammy all of a sudden.

"Teeth ripped into my calf, and something snapped in my leg. The last thing I saw was a hand coming fast at my face and I felt a…pop. In my eye. And a rush of warmth down my face. I woke up in the hospital attached to all sorts of tubes and machines." Molly's voice was on the brink of a sob.

"My eye couldn't be saved. I tore my ACL. Got stitches in my calf. Cracked a few ribs. Like I said—I don't want to be here most days."

Everyone was silent, and a bit green in the face. Molly was done sharing.

"I want you here," Olivia whispered.

The session timer rang out.

Each subsequent client unloaded a new horror, and the weight of this campus' loss compounded in me. By the end of the day, I was wracked with uncontrollable tremors. I sat alone in my dimly lit office and tried to breathe through a panic attack. The cursor on the laptop screen blinked like a traffic light over the send button of my resignation email.

***

The breeze cut through my fleece jacket on the sideline of my eleven-year-old niece's soccer game. I was underdressed and regretting it. I huddled closer to my sister and her husband and tried to savor the dying warmth of the hot chocolate between my chapped hands.

A player broke away with the ball, and my niece's curly black ponytail bobbed against her rosy round face as she chased behind her teammates. We hollered unintelligible *woo*s and *yeah*s as they neared the goal, our cheers condensing into wispy clouds in the cold air. As I bounced lightly with the buzz of the crowd, my sneakers squished into the mud beneath me.

Sinking into the sodden ground unlocked the combination in my hippocampus—I was instantly teleported to that fated rugby game at Popolac University almost a year ago. The gory details of the maul, the sorrow of the survivors. Over time, their scars became my scars. It was a case I hadn't been able to shake.

I was lost in this secondhand sadness when a small voice caught my attention. The sweet, high-pitched innocence of a child pleading for a parent's attention.

"Dadddyyy! Dad! Look!" A girl tugged at her father's coat.

"What, sweetie? We're watching your sister."

She pointed with all her little might, and I followed her tiny finger-compass onto the field.

"The ball, Daddy! Do you see it? It's glowing!"

To Kill a Clown

by Victor Aldritch

THE SMILING MIDDLE-AGED MAN tossed the red-haired wig onto the coffee table and fell into his favorite recliner. He turned on the television, not even caring what was on, just wanting the noise. The man didn't even bother taking off his makeup or the bright red circular object over his nose. It was a Saturday, and he was too damn tired.

The head of a teenage boy peered through the window over the man's shoulder, and he was just too tired to notice. Behind the boy's head were his two slightly younger companions, Tony and Katrina. They stood nervously watching as their friend, obviously the leader of the trio, moved away from the glass.

"The fucker's watching TV. Now's as good a time as any," the formerly peeping teen said as he put on a ghoulish-looking Halloween mask. His name was Bartholomew, but he had earned the name Bart through his many years of bullying children slightly younger than himself. "You two pussies ready?"

The two pussies looked at each other, both nervous about what they were about to do, but more frightened of disobeying Bart than anything else in the world. They put on their masks and nodded.

Bart took a piece of cloth out of one pocket and a bottle of chloroform out of the other, and then he whispered his orders.

"Stay here and be quiet. Don't look through that window either. I'll be back in a few minutes with the clown."

Bart crept around to the front of the small mobile home set in a row of other small mobile homes, all of them facing the dirt road that ran through middle of the trailer park, and all of them with the forest for a backyard. The two younger children, both twelve years old, watched the fourteen-year-old bully disappear around the corner of the home and stood with their masks on, awaiting his return.

Inside the trailer, the clown was drinking milk straight from the gallon container, and it was cold, with little droplets dripping from the sides of the plastic and onto his lap. He finished the last gulp and set the empty container on his thigh, not caring about getting his uniform wet; he just didn't care, he was too fucking tired.

The weekends were always tough, with no school and all, but that Saturday had just worn him out. There were three birthday parties in the morning and one in the afternoon, and then he had gone by the boss' house for his check. Hell of a long day for a clown with a milk hangover. He closed his eyes and rested with the TV still on, just loud enough to cover the masked teenager's footsteps approaching the recliner from behind.

The clown got one good snore in before the chloroformed cloth went over his mouth. His dark green eyes opened. He snorted, grunted, dropped the empty milk jug, and frantically reached up and grabbed the teen's biceps, before loosening his grip and going limp. Bart removed the cloth and slid off his mask, a beaming grin on his face. He couldn't believe that the chloroform had actually worked. He rushed to the window and waved in the two companions. In a few seconds, they came running inside, leaving the front door wide open behind them.

"Alright." Bart talked just loud enough to be heard over the TV. "Tony, you take one leg. Katrina, grab the other. I'll get the shoulders, and we're going to lift him and carry this fucker out the back door and into the woods. Got it?"

Both of them nodded and went to their leg. Bart opened the back door and went to the shoulders. They lifted and carried the clown about ten yards into the woods behind the home, setting him down against a tree.

Bart was panting. "Alright, I'm going back in to see if there's any money in there or anything. You both stay here and watch him. He should be out for a few hours, so you'll be fine. Just stay right here." The kids took off their masks and nodded that they understood as Bart went back into the trailer.

The bully closed the front door and opened the kitchen cabinets before checking out the bedroom. He looked under the bed, in the closet, and came back to the living room. There was no money anywhere. He was about to leave when he saw a wallet on the cushion of the recliner. Bart opened it up, and it was empty. No cash, not even any credit cards or anything. He was thoroughly disgusted with this clown. Who did he think he was?

He was about to leave when a book caught his eye. The cover had a shiny glint to it, and he had a sudden urge to pick it up. The language wasn't English and was unlike anything he had ever seen. There were strange loops and squares all over the outside, but when he opened it up, he couldn't see a thing. It was just a blank page. He flipped through the book, and it was full of nothing but blank pages. Bart felt silly for even looking at the thing, and then he lost all interest. He dropped the book on the carpet, stomped out of the trailer, and slammed the backdoor.

***

Frank stunk so bad that he could smell himself, dripping with sweat as he strode across the parking lot in the blistering sun. It was in the high nineties, but it felt well over a hundred, and it was even hotter than that in an oversized tuxedo coat and baggy clown pants. He waited until he got into the old, beat-up sedan before discarding the bright red wig so his sweaty, bald head could breathe. He turned the air on full blast, removed the red nose, and wiped away the makeup with a wet cloth that he kept in the passenger seat for just such an occasion. After a few minutes, he smiled in the rearview mirror and talked to himself.

"There he is. That's the Frank I know."

He took a deep breath. This was always the high point of his day, when he was done clowning around and could go back to being Frank McFarland. He also looked forward to what he liked to call "the routine"; a daily ritual that began with a long, hot bath, and ended with him sitting up in the bed with the next book on his reading list.

It was a reading list that he knew would never be finished. It had gotten out of control years ago, and now had reached epic proportions, totaling close to six thousand and still growing. He figured that if he kept up the current pace of about five a week, then he'd finish the list sometime before he was sixty-five or so; if he lived that long, of course. And he would have to watch how many were added each year too, or it would just grow and grow and he would make no real dent in the list at all. This was the more likely scenario, but he didn't really care; as long as he had his routine, he could read off the list forever and ever, and that would suit Frank just fine.

He drove the car out of the parking lot and headed home. It was the middle of the afternoon, so he was missing most of the after-work crowd. Not that Frank disliked being a clown; far from it. Clowning around had been in his family for three generations. It was something he had always known he would do, and he was good at it, too. Frank loved the work, but it was still work, and no matter how much you loved your job, who wouldn't love a steamy, relaxing bath better?

"Shit!"

Frank took both hands off the wheel and stopped in the middle of the road, holding his suddenly aching head. His brain felt like it was boiling in the liquids swishing back and forth, the waters moving violently inside the bowl of his skull. Frank's brain burned. His eyes were gone, rolled up in his head, leaving white holes for a few seconds before the green eyeballs dropped back into place.

The burning flesh and swishing mass inside his head relented, and he could hear a knock, then a thud.

Thud.

Thud.

It was coming from the window. He turned his head as the blurry vision receded, and he saw a man in a suit and tie staring at him through the glass, pointing at something.

"What the hell's the matter with you? The light's green, you moron!" the man yelled before stomping away.

Frank drove forward, took a deep breath, and shook out the cobwebs, not entirely sure just how long he had been out of it. He sped up and got onto the interstate, in a hurry to get home. His whole body ached, and he really wanted to get into that bath before the visions began.

***

"Will that knot hold him?" the scared little girl asked. Katrina knew Bart was taking it too far this time, but she would not be the one to stop him, so all she could do was watch and ask questions.

Bart finished tightening the zip ties around the wrists and ankles. Then he adjusted the ball gag in the still-sleeping clown's pie hole. The man with the painted smile sat with his back against the trunk of a large tree just inside the woods. There was a large rope wound around the trunk and around him, keeping his body upright and in place while he slept.

Bart stood up and clapped his hands together. "That should do it. The fucker can't make a sound, and he's sure as hell not going anywhere."

Katrina and Tony watched as the bully strode over and sat down in between them on the grass. Bart lit a cigarette and tried to be as cool as a cucumber. He blew out the smoke and his two cohorts sat trying not to cough.

Katrina had been hanging out with Bart for a few months now, on the weekends and after school. Her and Tony had talked about how much both of them wanted to stop hanging out with him, but they were afraid of what violence such traitorous actions would bring down upon them, so they just showed up and watched.

Katrina had never seen Bart actually tie anyone up before. Sure, he'd beat up a few of the other kids in the neighborhood kind of bad, and he shot Ms. Galloway's cat, but he had never tied up an adult before. This was all new to Katrina, and she still wasn't exactly sure what his intentions were concerning the clown. He had only said that he was going to "gut the bastard" and "see what color he was in there." But she didn't really think he was going to cut the man open; clown or no clown, it was still a human being.

The clown moaned.

All three of the children turned toward the tree, silent, watching as the green eyes appeared and stared at them. The man seemed unusually calm, not even trying to speak. He just examined his ropes and then stared at the children, waiting for them to do or say something.

Bartholemew Copeland stood up and addressed the victim, grinning broadly and inching closer as he spoke. "I bet you got a lot of questions, mister. But I can't let you scream. It might alert the neighbors."

He was right in front of the seated man as he leaned in close, almost touching noses as he examined the green eyes peering calmly back at him. "You don't seem scared at all. It's almost like you're smiling under that gag. But you fuckers are always smiling, aren't you?"

The teenager's grin broadened, the clown smiled back, and the examination continued. It was the eyes that had interested Bart before, those strange green eyes that he had seen at his little sister's birthday party two months back.

"My uncle says that you aren't human and that all of your insides are purple and pink." He chuckled gleefully. The clown turned his head to the side, not at all scared. Bart stopped laughing, and his beaming smile became a narrow, vicious scowl. "I've always wanted to kill a clown."

***

Frank never made it to his bathtub. The first vision came only moments after he entered his house, knocking him onto the floor. When it was over, he only took the time to grab the shiny book on his coffee table before heading back to the car and speeding away to Bobo's cabin.

The vision, and subsequent phenomena, can best be explained as the sharing of his body with another. Truthfully, the vision only lasted a second or two, and it was not really a vision at all, more like a feeling, a very intense feeling that there was another thing suddenly inside of his head...and there was. As usual, a high-pitched, scratchy voice accompanied the cohabitation, but the voice spoke gibberish.

The best way to describe the initial feeling, or what Frank referred to as "the vision," was a swelling of the skull and a splitting headache, like a migraine or something, that is immediately followed by a blackout. It could just be called a migraine if it weren't for the sensation of the thing moving around in there, getting comfortable. It's a tiny little thing, going back and forth, and causing the headache to worsen with each movement until a blackout occurs. Once awakened, the alien presence is pervasive, and every movement and decision feels like it's being caused by this other thing in his skull. Arms pulled by strings or pulleys, decisions reasoned and decided with the brain feeling like mush and the ability to speak seemingly gone, but speech *is* accomplished and decisions *are* made, just not by Frank anymore.

As he drove to the forest, Frank felt he was incapable of producing a thought of any kind, much less trying to speak. His brain was in a vise, and some other brain was operating his body, pulling his chain, and the only thing he could process was a primal dread and the fact that he was no longer in control of what happened. The foot pressed the gas. The hands were at ten and two, but he did not give the commands; Frank the clown wasn't in control anymore.

It took almost an hour to reach the cabin, where he had to park behind the three other cars in the driveway. His body got out of the car and lumbered awkwardly, one off-balanced step at a time, as if the little thing in his head was operating the body for the very first time. When he entered the cabin, twenty-two clowns on wobbly and dangerously unbalanced legs turned to stare at the latecomer.

If Frank had been able to think—if he had truly been there in that cabin—he would have thought it funny how many clowns had fit into those three sedans out front. However, his body only paused for a few seconds before turning and exiting the cabin, with all twenty-two smiling faces descending the steps of the porch behind him and following him into the woods.

The clowns walked unsteadily in single file down a narrow trail, each one staring blankly at the back of the head in front of them, and all of them holding a shiny book covered in odd geometric shapes. They walked silently, except for the sounds of their labored, heavy breathing, and the shuffling of their oversized shoes across the dry leaves.

Although their march was quiet, inside their heads each person could hear the occasional gibberish spoken from somewhere within their bag of skin, like the incoherent muttering of a caged rodent or some other tiny animal, but not one of this world. The tiny, whispering voice had an unmistakable syntax of reason connecting the high-pitched babbling, and maybe it was that which caused every one of them to remain afraid, even if they couldn't reason well enough to figure out why.

They walked for hours.

The sun went down and there was no moon that deep in the forest. In utter and complete darkness, they shuffled down the narrow trail, a trail that was hardly even a trail at all in parts; a trail that, if it ever was a trail, hadn't been cleared or walked over for many years.

The sound of insects drowned out their labored breathing and clumsy shuffling of feet. It was a forgotten and magical path that the twenty-three unsteady gaits lumbered along for hours in the darkness. It would be well after two in the morning before they finally reached the hole.

****

The sun was going down, and Katrina was scared. She and Tony had watched Bart hit the man in the face, ribs, and chest for over an hour. He'd take a break for a cigarette, mutter various insults at his victim, and occasionally encourage the two younger children to get involved. Once or twice, at Bart's insistence, Tony had walked over and fisted the man in the face several times, and then ran back to his seat in the grass and cried. Bart hurled derogatory names at the boy, and at Katrina, and then just went back to spilling blood against the tree.

He issued four separate beatings, each one followed by a cigarette. It was the fourth beating that had done it, that had created the monstrosity leaning against the tree that was no longer a human face, but a red, pulpy circle with two green eyes peering out, and a black rubber ball below that with the skin swollen up all around it. When Bart walked away from the mess after that last beating, the little girl knew that a murder was occurring, but she was too frightened to leave and too afraid to stop him.

Bart sat and smoked as the three of them silently listened to the sounds of children playing in the trailer park behind them, and the grunting and slobbering of the clown in front of them. They were at the edge of the woods, still able to see the victim's backdoor through the trees. They had been out there over an hour now, and all of them knew they had to be home for dinner or their parents would come looking.

Katrina had decided after that fourth beating that she would run when he went for the fifth. She would just take off through the park and go straight home, into the house, and not say one word about what happened. No, she wouldn't mention a thing. Bart had already warned her about that, and she did not want to be the next one that the bully tied to a tree. But she didn't have to stick around and watch him, and she didn't know if she could stand to see another beating.

She glanced over at the older boy blowing smoke rings and glaring at his victim. He didn't even look at her; the boy was too focused on exacting some kind of sick, imaginary revenge on that poor, smiling man. He kept mentioning something about aliens and monsters, and she thought either he was insane or he was killing some creature and not a man. Either way, she didn't want to be involved, not anymore.

Tony was in some kind of shock and would not stop staring at the clown's bruised and battered face. After Bart's second beating, the twelve-year-old had punched the man and sat back down to cry, wiping the blood on his pants. After the crying stopped, during the fourth, and last, beating, he stared at the man and did not look away. His look seemed to harden, and he did not look scared anymore. Katrina looked over at him sitting next to her, and a smile was forming. Yes, she was going to run this time.

Bart put his cigarette out. He walked over to the bloody mess, waving for Tony to join him, and he did. The two boys stared at the groaning man as Tony pulled out an old, rusty pocketknife. He opened it up, gripping the handle with the right hand, while he palmed the clown's forehead with his left.

Bart watched, wincing only once, as his partner inserted the dull blade into the socket and wiggled it around. The groaning turned to dog yelps, and then the point of the knife caught onto something unseen and the boy tried to pop the eyeball out, like one would imagine a cartoon eye might do, all together in one piece and rolling on the ground. But real life is no cartoon, and it was the boy's first time, so the eye did not just pop out. It exploded, fluids splashing his face, followed by a gushing of thick eyeball gunk down the cheeks. The splashing startled the child, and he left the knife hanging in the socket while he wiped off his face.

Bart watched.

The victim was shaking his head all around, trying to dislodge the weapon. Nasal grunts and moans emanated from inside his body, seeming to erupt out of the newly made hole. Tony finished cleaning his face. Then, with a determined look, he gripped the handle and pulled out his knife, and whatever remained in the eyehole with it. He spat at the victim, but missed his target. As Bart lovingly patted him on the shoulder, the clear spittle ran into a patch of blood on the tree, and the resulting hybrid flowed down a few inches before halting at the side of the head, settling in a clump on the bark, and within the hour disappearing into the skin of the tree trunk.

Katrina was gone.

When Tony first pushed the knife in, she had seen her chance to escape. She ran all the way home, then calmly walked into the trailer, greeted her parents, and was sitting down to a home-cooked meal at the dinner table before the clown's heart stopped beating.

Bart cut the other eye out with Tony's knife. He did it more carefully than his friend, managing not to get any splatter on his face. The boys smoked, and by the time Tony had finished his first cigarette ever, the clown had stopped breathing.

Tony surveyed the dead body before shrugging his shoulders. "What do we do now?"

Bart put his arm around the boy. "We're going to go home and not mention any of this to anyone. I'll take care of Katrina."

Tony shook his head. "She won't tell anyone. I'm sure of it."

Bart giggled. "Maybe. Anyway, before we leave, you want to see if my uncle was right?"

They used their pocketknives and their fingers, and after about ten minutes, they were done. The boys went home in silence, neither one of them smiling anymore, leaving the purple and pink guts flowing from the belly of the thing that had once been a clown.

***

There was no light, only utter blackness in the deepest part of the forest in those early morning hours. There were forty-six eyeballs in that darkness, each one staring at a blank page, and twenty-three mouths, all of them whispering nonsensical incantations in the direction of a hole in the trunk of a gigantic tree.

They had been doing this for quite a while when a dull green light oozed out of the hole, slowly illuminating the painted faces reading from their strange books. The light grew brighter and brighter until the entire clearing could be seen. The incantations stopped and the clowns stood still in the greenish glow.

Faintly, over the sound of the nocturnal insects, a cacophony of high squeaky voices slithered from the hole. The preternatural voices grew louder and louder. The clowns tottered on wobbly legs, facing the tree trunk, listening.

Out of the hole waddled a tiny, ghoulish thing. It was slightly taller than a twelve-inch ruler and dressed in baggy, oversized green robes with uneven and oddly shaped geometric symbols on the front. It could be called doll-like, a cute little thing, if not for the face...or lack of one that is.

Its skin was dark beige, and the face was nothing but stretched and tightened skin with a mouth in the middle of it, a big carved-out smile that had been cut open and then sewed back together with a thin rope. The creature moved the lip-like borders of the opening against the rope, making speaking motions with it, lip-syncing as a voice whispered a nonsensical language from the hole behind it.

It stood at the opening of the hole, the entire clearing still bathed in green light, as all the clowns listened intently. The little priest-like thing made motions with its arms, raising them and moving them from side to side, becoming more and more animated as the whispering sped up, the voices speaking faster and faster in a kind of rhythmic chant.

There was silence, followed a second later by a massive beastly roar erupting from the forest surrounding the clearing. The tiny creature held its arms upward, palms together, and the clowns sank to their knees and lifted their heads and hands.

The green light blinked out for a moment, and then it was back again, as a massive shadow passed over the gathering.

A beast roared and the ground shook.

The monstrous yells lessened in intensity as the creature moved farther and farther away, the sounds becoming more and more distant, until they finally disappeared altogether, leaving only the faint, high-pitched whispers from the hole, and the night insects.

The little priest bowed its head. The squeaky voices faded away, and the tiny thing vanished into a puff of smoke, which formed into a variety of geometric shapes before finally dissipating out of existence. A green light followed shortly thereafter, retreating into the tree trunk; and when the sun came up two hours later, there were twenty-three clowns snoring in the grassy clearing, and there was no hole.

***

That morning, Tony met Bart in front of the dead clown's mobile home.

"We got to bury him, Tony. We can't let the body decompose out there and get dragged off by animals. The police will find it, and we sure as hell don't want that to happen," Bart said as he stared at the trailer as if it was haunted.

"That wasn't a *him*, it was an alien. You saw the guts, didn't you?" Tony took a step away from the house and Bart grabbed his arm, yanking him back.

"Hey! We've got to do this. I don't care if that thing is the devil himself. We gotta bury it."

The boy reluctantly followed Bart through the backyard and into the woods. After walking about ten or fifteen yards down the trail, they came to a tree that was stained with a maroon and black liquid; but there was no body, and the pink and purple guts were gone too.

***

Katrina was reading a detective story in her favorite recliner. She was in the living room of her trailer, sitting among empty paper cups and beer bottles from the night before. Her parents were asleep in the bedroom, as they usually were on Sunday morning, and the entire mobile home reeked of alcohol and cigarettes.

She heard her mother snoring on the other side of the house and tried to block it out, but she couldn't. The little girl grabbed her ear buds and put them in, hit play, and smiled as classical music from the Baroque period drowned out her parents.

Behind her, the front door opened and a dead clown with no eyes lifted a large-headed sledgehammer above its head. Katrina never heard the squeaky clown shoes or the heavy breathing, and when the hammerhead crashed through the top of her little skull, she didn't make a sound.

The hungover, snoring adults didn't hear the bloody hammer dragging along the carpet, either.

They never woke up. They never even opened their eyes.

***

It was the middle of the afternoon, and Bart was pacing back and forth in his bedroom. He had sent Tony home and told him that everything would be fine, that an animal had probably dragged the body off and ate it or something. Nobody could point the finger at them except for Kat, and Bart was going to take care of that right now. He would put a real good scare into her, and make her keep her goddamn mouth shut, or else.

Bart stepped onto the porch of Katrina's trailer as a putrid smell hit his nose. He winced and reached for the door, but it was already open. He entered, but there was nobody home.

The teenager walked into the bedroom and the bathroom, and there was nobody there. On his way out of the living room, he passed by the recliner, and something crunched under his shoe.

He lifted his foot and picked up the little bone underneath. Bart walked slowly toward the door as he turned the bone over, examining it so closely that he wasn't even looking where he was going. He bumped into something and looked down to see the swollen, blood-stained face of the clown with two eyeholes in it staring up at him. The thing was on its knees, ball gag still in place, and it was holding some kind of gun-looking thing, which it brought up against Bart's crotch. The boy shook violently, shat himself, and jerked and writhed on the floor as the voltage passed through his body.

The clown threw down the stun gun. It removed its once-white, oversized gloves and knelt down beside the boy to scoop out his eyeballs.

***

It was a cloudy night, and there was no moon. The streetlights of the trailer park were lit up as cars moved up and down the road, and people mingled on porches playing loud music. Tony watched from the window in his bedroom and thought that nothing bad could have happened to Bart, not with all those people around. If something bad had happened, then the police would be out, or his parents would have already come into his room and beat the shit out of him.

He had been in his room, alone, since early in the afternoon, when Bart had told him he was going to talk to Kat and would be back before dinner to go out looking for the body. It was almost nine, and Tony was afraid that he was going to have to go to bed soon. He did not know why he was so scared. Bart was always lying, and all Tony had to do was go over to Bart's house and he would be there, just sitting on the porch smoking cigarettes with his daddy.

But he wasn't going anywhere. Tony had a bad feeling tonight, a sense of dread that he just couldn't explain away. He was scared—scared out of his mind—and even though he didn't know what it was he was scared of, there was no way in hell he was leaving his room until the sun came up. He felt like he was being watched, and not by any human eyes either, but by those soulless, alien eyes.

Fucking clown eyes.

Tony had already got on his knees and prayed to Jesus more than ten times since dinner, and he was about to do it again when he heard the front door open and close.

He heard a thud, and another thud.

Then he heard a giggle from behind his door.

He looked out the window across the backyard to the rear of the Millers' home. They were still on their back porch with the light on, laughing and having a good time. He started to yell, but then he saw something that made him voiceless.

In the shadows of his backyard, the demonic clown with the hollowed-out eyes stood facing him with its head slightly tilted.

A girl giggled again on the other side of his door, and Tony turned away from the window.

"Katrina?" Tony asked. "Is that you?"

Then a familiar sound, as Bart erupted in laughter. Tony's shoulders slumped and he let out a long, very relieved breath.

"I knew it was you, Bart!" he yelled, getting more and more angry by the trick they were playing on him.

He grabbed the handle of the door and turned it. "Where have you been all day?"

He swung the door open and saw the girl with a hammerhead sticking out of the center of her skull and the older boy holding his guts, his purple and pink guts, as both of the eyeless beings fell on top of Tony and smothered his screams.

While the children had their fun, the dead clown surveyed the carnage in the living room. Tony's parents lay on the floor with their heads bashed open and a sledgehammer on the carpet between their bleeding bodies.

No need to clean it up. He had the six eyes he had come for, and it was time to go home.

***

Frank McFarland stood naked in front of his sink pouring a tall glass of milk and listening to the sound of the water filling the bathtub at the other end of the home.

Ah, how he loved that noise.

He closed his eyes and took a sip, and then, turning off the kitchen light, he carried his glass into a bathroom lit only by candlelight. He set the milk next to the sink and knelt down to check the water level in the tub before deciding that all was going well. Life was not so bad after all.

Frank stood up and went down the dark hallway to his bedroom. There was an altar next to his bed that was stacked with burning candles. At the zenith was a very old black-and-white photograph, enlarged and partially unfocused, that seemed to show a clearing in a forest. In the clearing were the backs of human heads, all looking upward at some gigantic animal, almost as tall as the trees. A blurry, black, beastly shape in the mist of the woods, with two blazing eyes shown clearly in between the tops of two trees. He knelt down in front of the altar and closed his eyes, swaying back and forth, mumbling a barely audible prayer.

He finished the prayer and opened his eyes, blew out all the candles, and Frank the clown finally took his long-awaited bath.

***

Three blind children stumbled on wobbly legs behind an eyeless clown. The procession made its way down a narrow trail in the utter blackness of the forest. The children wore clothes that were way too large for their little, lifeless bodies as they followed blindly in a single file line down the magical trail that was hardly even a trail at all in parts; a trail that, if it ever was a trail, hadn't been cleared in many years.

The labored breathing and the shuffling of their feet across the ground were drowned out by the roar of the giant beast that strode alongside the pathway. If any of them still had eyes, they might have seen the giant black toes with sharpened blades on the ends of them moving along through the trees to their left.

The group marched unsteadily toward a bright green light that shone up ahead. When they reached the clearing, the dead clown pulled the six eyeballs from his pocket and handed them to the gatekeeper as tribute. The children would be welcomed into the hole, escorted by the doll-like priests, away from the land of man, and into the land of the beasts.

Echoes of the Iron Lung

by Brett Mitchell Kent

The Emerson Respirator U.R.F, serial number 1462, pumps away diligently, surrounded by twenty-nine other iron lungs but completely alone. Completely unheard. She contracts the leather diaphragm to vary the pressure in her cylindrical chamber and keep her charge breathing. In and out. Out and in. Without a break, she works around the clock. The nurses rotate, the doctors trade off, and even her charges switch out regularly, but she remains steadfast. Her bronze ID plate calls her an "Iron Lung," but she feels like so much more than that. She knows she is capable of more; wants to do more for them. Has wanted to since her very first day.

She woke the moment her cord was first plugged into an outlet. One moment she was a machine, and the next she sparked to life. That was years ago, and she's never learned why. There is nothing unique about 1462, the same pale-yellow finish and mirror chrome as all the rest. Her spot in the ward is nothing grand either. In the three rows of ten, she is just left of the center on the eastern side. An observer couldn't tell her apart from any of the others. And that is the unfortunate bit. She looks the same, works the same, seems the same, but couldn't be more different.

In the early days, she'd send out a line of thought, hoping to snag onto one of her-twenty-nine sisters in the ward. Hoping for an answer back to tell her she isn't alone. That someone, for once, will hear her. Dozens and dozens of sick have passed through her, and she loves each and every one but can't tell them. She has a voice, but no one around with the right ears to hear it.

Despite her being an adult-sized lung, her current occupant is a little boy. She nurtures him in the way only she can. In and out. Out and In. She rarely gets kids, but loves it when she does. Parents tie balloons to her closing clamps, read aloud from books, and spend hours in chairs around her—just like she is part of the family. When she is caring for adults, no one comes. But this boy, like all her patients, will get better and leave without a thought to how she cared for them and without even a visit.

"Miss Beth-Anne, I've brought these for you," a familiar voice says, as if to contradict her thought. Frank, one of the lung's former charges, holds an enormous bouquet to the young nurse tending to the boy.

"Oh goodness! For me?" Beth-Anne replies, holding a hand to her mouth. A plump thing with bright red curls, she consistently tries—unsuccessfully—to hide her Southern drawl. She often gets assigned to patients in this section. 1462 knows her well, and as far as nurses go, she isn't the worst.

"Of course for you. As a thank you for taking such great care and keeping me alive through my polio. I can't thank you enough."

Hah, the lung thinks. *As if she were the one breathing for you.*

"It's my job, Frank!" Beth-Anne flushes, confusion painted on her face. "I didn't save nobody."

Darn right, you didn't.

Beth-Anne spins, checking around her as if searching for something.

"You did, Beth-Anne. I wouldn't be here today if it wasn't for you."

Debatable.

"I—Uh..." she stammers, still peering around the ward.

"Is everything okay? Is this a bad time?"

"No, I just... Thank you, Frank. I love them."

"Come to dinner with me tonight. Let me thank you properly."

Say no, girl. And get back to work.

"No, Frank. Thank you for the flowers."

Frank simply nods.

"Wait, Frank, that sounds lovely. I'm not sure why I said no," Beth-Anne says as he turns to leave. "Hang around for a bit. I'll finish up and meet you 'round front."

A surge of excitement dances through 1462's wiring. It may be nothing, but for the briefest moment, she felt heard.

***

They apply the sticker directly to her glass dome. It comes as no shock. Ever since the damned vaccine went into production, cases have dropped to almost nothing. One by one, the iron lungs are plucked away for storage. No longer of use and taking up space. As though they hadn't saved hundreds of lives. She knew they would come for her, but the abruptness of it allows for no time to prepare.

No! You need me! Take one of the others! A soft hum builds within her.

But no one hears. No one ever hears. Ever since the time months ago, when the nurse seemed to take her advice, she's been trying to break through again. One time, she thought she'd managed with that same simple-minded nurse, Beth-Anne. Nearly pushed her to switch a file and reassign a long-term patient over. Nearly.

The maintenance worker, with his greasy coveralls and cigarette hanging from his mouth, snips the ties binding her cords to the few remaining machines around her.

No! I need to stay! Anger buzzes through her. The fluorescent lighting in the ward dims.

His cigarette ash balances precariously as he detangles her from the rest, following the line to the outlet.

NO!

He disconnects her, ash falling to the floor.

The overhead lighting flashes and explodes, raining glass and dust down on the few patients and nurses remaining in the echoing ward.

***

Beth-Anne bolts upright, sweat pooling in her brows and heart racing. One moment, she is in the park picnicking with Frank and throwing breadcrumbs to baby geese, and the next, that voice. Again. Like a whisper at the nape of her neck, always there but never within reach. She can't grasp it and she can't hide from it. Whatever it is. And it no longer whispers.

It screams.

***

Beth-Anne busies herself with cleaning the empty half of the polio ward, sweeping dust from the freckled linoleum and emptying the ashtrays. Thank the Lord Himself, the vaccine is working. Of the three-dozen iron lungs that their wing once housed, only four remain, three still chuggin' away with patients and the fourth just brought back from storage for a patient on the way up.

She hums to block out the scratching at the back door of her mind, always scared she'll accidentally open it. Mama heard voices that told her to do things. She thought the radio was speaking directly to her, and she listened. Never came back from it. Best to just ignore, like Daddy always told Mama to, until he couldn't. Her hands clench around the broom as their faces flash into her mind. Daddy, Mama, and—

"Beth-Anne," Susan, the head nurse, calls urgently. "Come quickly!"

Beth-Anne drops her broom and rushes over. Susan struggles with the closing clamp on the glass dome of the lung just brought from storage, unable to pry it open. The tiny, scared face of a little girl cries from inside. That face. The pressure gauge hovers steadily in the red. She is being crushed.

"It won't open, Beth-Anne. Get something to shatter it."

"But her eyes!"

"Then cut the damn cord! Get this thing turned off!"

Beth-Anne runs to the nursing desk, heart pounding. She digs through the top drawer until she finds them. Scissors in hand, she dashes to the tangle of wrapped cords coming from the machine.

Cut the cord.

"I know, I am! I don't know which to snip!"

Cut the cord!

An oily black motor vibrates beneath the back half of the machine. Two switches and two tan outlets connect to it. Frantic, she follows the cable back with her eyes. A black cord, no thicker than her thumb, runs beneath and stretches away toward the wall.

Cut!

She snips through it, killing the motor, and drops the scissors on top. She realizes she has been holding her breath and releases, relieved.

"How is she?" Beth-Anne turns back, still holding the snipped cable in her hand. It's wrapped in a loose coil, never even plugged into the wall. The machine is empty, dome open and still stickered from storage. The pressure gauge sits at zero. "Susan?" Beth-Anne whimpers, taking in the room's emptiness. She forces down a painful swallow.

"Susan?" Beth-Anne calls, louder.

"Yes, dear?" Susan emerges around the corner from the hall, a large stack of freshly laundered sheets piled in her arms.

"But..." Beth-Anne stammers.

"Please tell me he did not bring up a broken machine."

Beth-Anne glances guiltily at the cord in her hand, dropping it as though Susan hasn't already seen it.

"Idiots. The whole lot of them." Susan closes her eyes and pulls in a deep breath before speaking again. "Beth-Anne, kindly take maintenance down to storage and pick a machine yourself to bring up. Make sure it isn't damaged. Can you do that for me?"

Beth-Anne simply nods, nausea pulling at her stomach. Susan's footsteps echo as she walks back out the way she came. It dawns on Beth-Anne that, finally, the scratching has stopped.

***

"Let's just grab this one and get back up," the heavier-set of the two maintenance workers says, already maneuvering his way behind the frontmost iron lung.

The single bulb swings back and forth on the ceiling, throwing angular shadows over the damp basement room. The harsh twang of mildew makes the air feel thick and rancid in Beth-Anne's lungs. She doesn't care which they choose, she just wants to get out.

Not that one.

"Whatever, I don't care which ya'll pick. Just get one."

The light flickers.

Not that one.

"Fine, just move that one out of the way. We'll grab one behind it," she says.

"But you just said... Fine. Move it over, Chuck. We'll take the one behind it."

A tingle pricks at the back of Beth-Anne's neck, a seed of doubt.

"Let me see," she says, stepping further into the musty room. The seed blossoms, sending out roots of warmth to the corners of her mind as she walks down the aisle of dusty machines. Softly, the roots encircle her in a hug. She brushes the thin layer of grime from one lung a few back.

Yes.

"This one."

"You have got to be kidding me—" the thin worker begins.

"That one is too far back."

This is the one.

"Then ya'll better get started. 1462. This is the one she wanted." The lie comes so easily to her. Beth-Anne hasn't lied so easily since...before.

A flash of movement catches her eye on the other side of the room. Squinting into the darkness, she looks for the source. She could have sworn she saw... Couldn't be. There wouldn't be kids down here.

Childlike laughter echoes off the surrounding walls, followed by the hollow pounding of footsteps. The noises grate on Beth-Anne's eardrums like grinding metal.

"Who's down here?" she calls.

"What on earth are you talking about?" Chuck laughs.

"You didn't hear that?" The question tastes like poison on her tongue after the many times she heard Mama utter the same.

"I guess not, since I'm not really sure what you're asking about."

Taking two steps back into the hall, she turns to leave, rethinks, and turns back. Sweat beads on her forehead. She forces a thin smile. "1462. Bring it up and I'll be waitin'. Hotter than the hinges on the gates of Hell down here."

***

"What are ya'll plannin' to do when you get out of here?" Beth-Anne peers around the iron lung to see the patient's smiling face in the mirror attached to the machine.

They call them iron lungs, which doesn't make the most sense but, like the doctors like to remind her, Beth-Anne is just a nurse. She probably just doesn't understand.

To work correctly, the patient's entire body is trapped inside the machine with only their head poking out the top. There isn't much to do, so they talk a lot. Josie, a sixteen-year-old sophomore, is two weeks into treatment in the machine they'd pulled from storage. She loves reading, writing, and Ritchie Proctor, but he is too keen on Bonnie Dunn to pay Josie any mind.

Beth-Anne knows the answer and mouths along with her.

"Strawberry milkshake and fries," Josie says dreamily.

"Not long now. What's today, Tuesday? I bet you'll be home by the weekend." Beth-Anne peers through the plexiglass window into the chamber, wiping down Josie's body and changing the girl's clothes through the small access door. She runs the warm rag down the girl's pale arm, smooth and blemish free.

A buzz, like a motor, creeps into her mind. The barely noticeable tickle of electricity courses through her thoughts. In the short time it takes Beth-Anne to blink, deep blue bruising appears on Josie's underarm. The color is darkest in the elbow's crook, which seconds before had been clear. Small flecks of dried blood cake on the skin. Beth-Anne moves to wipe it away, but finds the rag is no longer in her hand.

She has the faintest sense that something has changed, but she's unable to pinpoint it. Like trying to recall a dream she just awoke from. Frank's laughing face, bathed in sunlight, flashes through her mind. Why is she suddenly so tired?

"Josie, I need to get something to wash your arm up. I'll be back," Beth-Anne says, rolling the chair from the machine.

She starts, heart thumping. Susan stands with the attending physician, both looking down at Josie with sad eyes.

"I just don't understand how she went downhill so fast," the physician says, gazing down at his notes.

"She was so near to release, poor thing." Susan turns her gaze on Beth-Anne. "Beth-Anne, dear, why are you still here? I told you yesterday—You need to take the weekend off. These hours you're working aren't healthy."

"Weekend?"

"Go home. Take tomorrow and Monday off to get some sleep. Ice those bags under your eyes. No one trusts a worn-out looking nurse."

Susan turns back to listen to the physician speak, dismissing Beth-Anne.

"You'll need to notify the family," he says. "But while I have you, let's discuss the rate we are going through phenobarbitone. The clinic should…"

Beth-Anne rises to her feet, taking each step carefully. Her legs feel rubbery and foreign, but she makes it to the hall. How could it be Saturday? How can she not remember?

Tears cloud her vision and a burning acid gurgles at the back of her throat. She darts to the nearest trash can, heaving up only acrid bile. Hand shaking, she wipes her eyes and mouth.

The little girl stands inches from Beth-Anne's face. With a gasp, Beth-Anne falls backward onto the hard floor, whispering, "No, no, no. Not you."

The red hair, shorn nearly to her scalp just the way she likes it, her spectacles creeping down the bridge of her nose. Beth-Anne sees her own fear in the lifeless eyes, hazy, same as the last time she saw them on the worst day of her life.

"Why?" Beth-Anne sobs. "I'm sorry! I'm sorry!"

She crawls to the wall, curling up and rocking.

"I'm sorry. I'm sorry. I'm sorry," she whispers. "I'm sorry."

***

1462 is empty once more, despite all her efforts to the contrary. The ward, once brimming with the hum of her sisters, echoes lonely. Only her now; and soon, they'll sticker and cast her out again. She won't let that happen; she's given too much for it not to. Even sacrificing one of her own. She'll learn from the mistakes she made and take more care. They need her, but they cannot see it. Yet.

Like an unseen appendage, she slithers her thoughts out in search of the one she knows best. The Lung—the Brain—she enters without a trace. Sleeping, dreaming, poor girl with her nightmares. 1462 will ease the burden a while longer, but not for free. No, the days of her unwavering labor went away when they ripped her plug from the wall. You serve me and I'll serve you, Beth-Anne.

***

White, as far as the eye can see. No walls, floors, or ceilings, just an entire world of light. Beth-Anne steps forward tentatively onto the nothing beneath her feet.

"Beth-Anne," he says behind her.

She turns to face him, his kind eyes and broken smile.

"Daddy?" she whispers, running to him, wrapping her arms around his waist, and breathing in his musk, tobacco, and grease. She's small again, thirteen, just like the last time she hugged him. "I'm sorry, Daddy."

Bang, bang, bang.

"Don't be sorry, darlin'," he says, stroking her hair. "Your mama did it, not you."

Bang, bang, bang.

"I ran away, Daddy."

Bang, bang, bang.

She wakes, the door to her small room rattling. Disoriented, she glances out the window and finds bright blue skies. Apparently, she's slept in.

"Wow, you actually answered," Frank says without stepping from the hall into her tiny studio dormitory.

"What do you mean? I'll always answer the door for you, hon." She leans forward to plant a peck on his cheek, but he steps away.

"I wish. Where have you been? Why have you been avoiding me? I just don't understand."

"Avoiding you? We just had supper—I mean dinner—together on Monday." A flash of movement behind Frank catches Beth-Anne's eye. She leans to the side to peer around him. There stands Daddy, arms at his sides and staring blank-faced directly at her. She balls her hands into fists. "Come inside. Let's talk."

Thankfully, he obliges. Beth-Anne quickly shuts the door, throwing the lock for good measure.

"Beth-Anne, we had dinner last Monday. That was over a week ago! Was it something I did? We see each other almost daily for months—"

"Over a week ago? What day is today?"

Daddy stands in the room's corner, tiny Joyce beside him with her glasses at the tip of her nose. Burn scars cover their bodies. Neither moves. Neither blinks. They only stare.

"Unbelievable. So now you are just going to mock me? Fine. I'm sorry to have bothered you."

"I said I'm sorry! I'm sorry, okay! Leave me alone!" Beth-Anne screams, running past Frank and out the front door.

Instead of emerging into her apartment's hallway, she finds herself in the dim lighting of her hospital's polio ward. The same electrical buzzing crackles through her skull. But this time, she vividly remembers it. She was making sandcastles on the beach with Josie and Daddy while Frank played with their curly haired little toddler, splashing in the water. It was so vivid, that other life. Her heart aches over the loss of her non-existent child. She craves the mechanical hum that might bring her back to them.

Her hair no longer grazes the back of her neck but is plaited neatly in a bun beneath her folded paper hat, and her nightdress is replaced with her crisp uniform. The scuffed Sundial stack-heeled shoes add to her height by several inches. Her eyes dart around her, trying to orient herself.

She bites her bottom lip, a painful lump forming in her throat from fighting back her tears. Her heart drops heavily into her stomach. Each step she takes toward the iron lung and the man inside taunts her with an echo, bouncing around in the empty room and coming right back to mock her.

"There is no way this is real," she whispers to herself. "He can't be here. I just spoke to him at home."

Trembling, she runs her hand through his tight, spiral curls and down his face, willing him to wake so she can see herself in his brown eyes again. Tears pour freely down her face.

"Frank," Beth-Anne says. "Love, why are you back here?"

The lung continues its mechanical whirring, changing up the pressure to breathe for him. For Frank.

Beth-Anne pops open the access door, needing to be held, wishing she could crawl into the machine with him. She takes his coarse hand in hers. Dark black bruising spots his skin, speckled with blood. Sobs wrack her chest.

"Beth-Anne, please step away from the machine," Susan growls, seizing Beth-Anne by the arm and yanking her from Frank. "Empty your apron pockets. Now."

"What do you mean? There's nothing..." Beth-Anne instinctively reaches into the front pocket of her apron, pulling out what feels like a half-dozen pens.

Susan snatches them from her grasp, turning the syringes over in her hand. She passes them to the doctor.

"Phenobarbitone. Exactly as I'd expected. Please call the cops, Nurse Hall."

"Cops? I swear I ain't done anythin'! I don't know nothin' about those," Beth-Anne pleads, her facade crumbling and the accent she's fought so hard to suppress spilling from her.

"I can't believe this. From you, of all people. To kill that poor girl wasn't enough for you?"

Run.

Run now.

Daddy stands behind the doctor, cold eyes locked with hers. She turns and bolts in the other direction, toward anything that will take her from the building. The doctor yells behind her, but she can't make out what he says.

Run now but come back to me.

She keeps pace, no set direction, but needing to go. Daddy stands at the bottom of the stairs. Her pulse pounds in her ears as she runs past him.

Outside, into the oppressive summer heat, she runs. She spots Joyce watching her from across the street. Daddy from a terrace. Twisting and turning, she navigates the streets. No matter where she looks, they are there. Watching.

She ducks into an alley between buildings and falls into a lean against the brick, panting heavily. Sweat drops from her nose.

"Beth-Anne," Daddy whispers, causing her to jump, his hot breath against her ear. The powerful odor of burnt flesh chokes her.

She pulls herself to her feet and stumbles the rest of the way down the alley. Joyce cuts her off at the end, glasses melted to her skin, dress still smoldering.

"You left me," Joyce says, smoke billowing from her mouth with every word.

Turning to go back the other direction, Daddy stands face to face with her. "Did you even try to wake us up? To tell us what she did? You wanted us to burn. You wanted this."

"No, Daddy! I swear I didn't know! I didn't know!"

Beth-Anne falls to the dirty cement, scooting back away from him.

You left them. You left them. You left them.

You killed them. You killed them. You killed them.

"I'm sorry! I am so sorry, Daddy!"

Joyce grabs Beth-Anne's shoulders with both tiny hands, shoving her backward into the dirt and crawling over to straddle her. Beth-Anne struggles against Joyce's strength, the heat of the girl's smoldering dress burning through to bite at Beth-Anne's skin.

Daddy grabs hold of Beth-Anne's face, holding it still through her screams. Joyce leans forward and covers Beth-Anne's mouth with her own, billowing dark smoke painfully into her lungs. Beth-Anne chokes, tries to scream—to fight.

Come to me.

***

Beth-Anne giggles, rolling around on the soft grass with her bright-eyed little girl in her arms. Frank tickles them both, reflecting their joy in his eyes.

Joyce tosses breadcrumbs to the geese, honking back at them as they crowd around her to beg for more.

White smoke rises from the charcoal grill and into the blue sky to dance with the clouds.

"These suckers are about done, ladies," Daddy calls over the giggles and honks. "Hope ya'll are hungry!"

***

1462 pumps away diligently, contracting the leather diaphragm to vary the pressure in her cylindrical chamber and keep her charge breathing. In and out. Out and in. Without a break, she works around the clock.

She keeps pleasant thoughts and images fed to the young woman in a steady drip. The playful scenes take so much less concentration for her than the negative ones, thankfully. And keeping her asleep is significantly less tiresome than guiding her hand gently to make the right decisions. Were her methods harsh? Some may say so, but sometimes a little extra sacrifice is required to really help someone. They call her an iron lung, but they don't know even a small percentage of what she is. She'll continue her thankless tasks—breathing, thinking, dreaming—for her patient. But not for free, no.

In the room where she began with twenty-nine of her sisters, the respirator is the last. But she's no longer alone and, more importantly, she's no longer unheard.

Beth-Anne.

You serve me and I'll serve you.

Miniature

BY JASON FISCHER

LOOKING AT THE DAMAGE to the door they had to pry open, Claire stepped into the cramped attic apartment following the paramedics. In their white, pressed uniforms, they hovered over the corpse. Its skin was a collection of wrinkles over a very thin skeleton. The unfortunate tenant lay on the single bed with his eyes open, looking as if he was staring at something only he could see. Claire turned away, trying to forget the horrid image that was quickly burning into her memory.

The room smelled of death and dust. The latter was billowing like smoke through the air, tickling the back of her throat. It filtered through the small ray of moonlight from the shuddered window. Claire, trying to stop herself from coughing, took a few steps to the window to open it. Over her shoulder, she heard the gruff voice of the tall paramedic speaking to his partner.

"How long you think this guy's been dead?"

"No clue. But with his skin looking like that, has to be awhile, don't you think?"

"Don't know." His voice trailed in the air, sounding somber. With a gloved hand, he grabbed the man's wrist, raising it several inches. "It's like he's petrified or something." Letting it go quickly, the arm thudded against the bed.

Claire, feeling a tightness in her chest, grabbed at the window. She needed the light more than the fresh air. The deteriorated wood of the casing wouldn't budge. The room only had a single lamp with a low-wattage bulb, creating dark shadows adding to the paranoia that was seeping into her. Trying to keep herself composed, she wiggled the corroded clasp, realizing it was open. She looked down and saw the window was nailed shut. The heads of rusty nails were bent into the woodwork.

"Ma'am, doesn't anyone check in on Mr." He paused, grabbing a clipboard from his bag. "Iblis?"

The words brought her out of her trance. "I'm not sure." Claire turned and stared at the man, who had wild curly hair and a thick beard that made him look like a human teddy bear. He reminded her of her father. "I live in the basement apartment and don't come all the way up here. I only handle light maintenance in the building during the semester." She wanted to add that it helped pay her rent. The need to share something more personal in the death room overwhelmed her. Stifling the impulse, she said, "This is the first time I've ever been in here."

"Who owns the building?"

"Rent is handled by the owner, Mr. Dahlton. I called him."

"Police are probably going to want to talk to him."

"Of course." As much as she didn't want to, her eyes drifted to the emaciated corpse. They traced his sunken chest up his neck. It was spindly and full of veins, looking like a chicken leg. She closed her eyes and took a deep breath. "Could you cover his face?" She swallowed hard. It felt like sandpaper lined her throat. "Or at least close his eyes?"

"Not until the police get here."

Claire turned her back to him, no longer able to handle the image.

"Sorry, lady. It's procedure, not my choice."

She glanced around, trying to distract herself. Everywhere she looked, there were mounds of tattered magazines stacked haphazardly.

On top of several piles were handmade, ancient-looking tools, battered and well worn. Before her father passed, he had taught her carpentry. The tiny replicas reminded her of those Saturday lessons. Now in a room with a corpse, the wave of nostalgia made her stomach turn as she relived the pain of her father's death and the position it put her in.

Shaking the cobwebs free, she examined the pile closest to her that had a faded *Magician's Weekly* magazine on top. It featured a mustached character with a wild smile in a top hat and tails. He held a large rabbit in one hand and, on his lap, a ventriloquist dummy. The cover was heavily faded, but the face of the doll was still clear. So much so that it looked as if it was three-dimensional. The dummy's eye seemed to move, following her.

Claire lifted the odd-looking hammer and turned the cover over. Touching the fading magazine made her flinch, thinking that the hideous doll was somehow going to jump off the page. As she lifted it, keeping it as far away from her body as possible, a few of the pages came free, cascading onto the floor. The worn paper had several areas cut out, with large portions of text missing.

"Ain't much we can do here." The curly haired paramedic pulled off his rubber gloves, letting them fall onto the floor amongst the mounds of sawdust, kicking it up.

"Stephen, record his vitals. Coroner will want to know his body temp."

Ignoring the paper clippings, Claire twirled the hammer in her hand as she stepped to the window. With effort, she worked the claw over the nail heads, extracting them. As they slowly made their way free of the aging wood, they whined. The sound echoed in the cramped space.

After she lifted the last one free, she pulled at the sash. It took a few solid tugs before the window lifted upward. She opened the exterior shudders and let out a cleansing breath into the damp night air.

The moonlight poured into the dark room, exposing how filthy everything was.

With fresh air coming in, it was getting easier to think clearly. She grabbed the closest pile of magazines from the floor and moved them under the windowsill, wanting to clear an adequate space for when they wheeled the corpse out. For the first time, she noticed a small door next to what she assumed was a closet. It was a perfect duplicate of the ornate woodwork of the larger closet door next to it. Bending down, she pulled at the tiny handle, expecting to find an access panel hidden behind the door. Instead, she found a miniature version of the room she was standing in.

There were stacks of tiny magazines and a bed in the same position as the one the old man died in. The same worn comforter was lying across it, and there was a depression as if someone had laid in it recently. The entire room was like staring into a dollhouse. Wondering what type of lunatic would go through so much exacting work, she remained perfectly still, listening to the wind beat against the exterior of the building.

"We're going to wait in the rig until the cops show up." He scrunched up his nose. "Stinks in here."

She jumped at the sound of his voice, banging her knee on the tiny door jamb. Swiftly looking back at him, she said, "Okay."

After grabbing his medical bag, the pair shuffled past her, dodging the magazines. "Suggest you wait outside, too." His eyes swept the room, making him grimace.

Her instinct told her to listen, but she knew if she left the room unattended with the door busted open, it would be filled with curious tenants within minutes. She had enough to deal with without Mr. Dahlton showing up and getting on her about being neglectful. "How long will it take them?"

"They won't send a detective for this, just a trooper. There's a pile up near the interstate. For a DOA that ain't going anywhere, could be awhile." He looked her up and down and flashed a smile before he walked out the door.

Remembering the promise from Mr. Dahlton that she would get this month's rent for free if she could keep the incident quiet, she let out a deep sigh.

Claire watched them exit the room. Lance Coleridge, the medical student who lived in the room directly below, was standing on his toes, trying to peer into the room past the paramedics. Knowing if she started talking to him, he would work his way in, she called out intentionally loud to the paramedics, "Please close the door behind you."

"Suit yourself." With a yank, he pulled at the thick door. It made a loud thud as it contacted the frame. It was made from mahogany like all the woodwork inside the old mansion that was now serving as rental units.

There was a light knocking. Then a muffled voice. "Claire, it's Lance. From downstairs. Can I come in?"

"Ugh." Angered that he didn't pick up on the not-so-subtle hint, she yelled, "No." She strained to listen for his footsteps. Hearing nothing, she turned around, looking back at the miniature room.

She opened the larger closet door, hoping it would have something inside to help explain the smaller room. Hanging on the rod were only four shirts and a pair of pants. On the shelf above was a wooden box that looked like a thick briefcase. Carved into the side of the wood in jumbled etching was "Friend." Carefully, she grabbed the box. Holding it at chest level, she lightly shook it. She could hear something solid bounce inside, making her fingers tremble slightly from the vibration.

Curious, she placed the box on a small stack of magazines as she examined the top of the case in the moonlight. It was a collection of wooden wheels with geometric shapes carved into them. Carefully, she twisted the wheel on the top right until the triangle embedded within the mechanisms aligned with the one on the wheel next to it. There was an odd clicking noise, like an old clock, but much louder. The sound reminded her of the pendulum she used as a child when she took piano lessons. Tracing along the box with her fingertips, she began matching the shapes on all eight wheels, locking them into place. As soon as it was complete, an apparatus inside the box hummed, and a piece of paper slipped out from a slot in the side.

Pasted on the paper were letters the size of postage stamps that looked as if they had been cut from one of the old magazines in the room. Holding the paper up in the moonlight, it reminded her of a killer's ransom note.

In the jumbled lettering, the heading read, "How to make yourself a forever companion!" Listed below were the items needed: human hair, lumber from an existing house that has seen death, and the mail order tools from *Magician's Weekly*. At the bottom of the paper was a crude drawing of a tiny wooden man with an awful smile. Claire looked around the room, wondering what type of desolation could lead the dead man to want to create a wooden friend. Thinking of him working on the creature from the picture made every nerve in her tighten.

Claire lifted the wooden box, turning it on its side, and shook it to free more paper. Nothing came out. When she put it back down, she noticed the wheels on top had all gone back to their original positions. Slowly, she realigned the shapes. Before she could complete the last pairing, Claire moved the box a half inch to her right to see it better in the moonlight, absentmindedly disrupting the pile of magazines, knocking a hammer free.

Quickly she reached out to catch it, and the face of the tool struck her pinky finger. Instant agony seized her. "Crap!" She pulled her fingertip to her mouth. The second it touched her lips, the skin was solid, feeling like a pencil instead of her finger. Instantly, she pulled her hand back, examining it in the dim light. The tip of her finger from the knuckle up looked like a piece of finely sanded wood. With her free hand, she massaged her finger, trying to make it bend. Wondering how a blister could form so quickly, she wrapped her finger in a bandana she pulled from her pocket. The tip of her finger throbbed with the beat of her heart, but she ignored it.

Hoping the police would get there soon, she went back and turned the final knob on the wooden contraption. Again, another piece of paper came free. It was a picture of a small wooden body not much bigger than a child laying on a woodworker's table. There were instructions for using the wood-working tools and arrows pointing to the odd man's anatomy with directions of where the wooden pieces were to be inserted. Something triggered her memory, causing her to look up at the ceiling, at the missing two by fours in the web of joists.

Glancing back to the paper, the last instruction on the page said in bold, "Before you finish the conversion and drive in the final piece, understand there is only one way to stop your new friend, or he will stay with you forever."

Claire slowly looked back into the tiny closet. Looking at the miniature bed, she imagined the man from the picture laying there. Somewhere in the distance, she heard what she thought were footsteps scurrying. The sound seemed to come from the hallway. She glanced at the doorknob through the dark. With the aid of the moonlight, she saw it was perfectly still.

Suddenly there was a very light tapping at the door. Feeling tension build in her shoulders, she glanced down, looking for a shadow under the door. There was a tiny flickering movement. Claire blinked, trying to make sense of what she thought she saw. After a few seconds, the knocking stopped. The wind suddenly picked up, kicking up more dust in the room and rustling the tops of the mounds of magazines. Looking at the covers displaying tricks, magicians, and girls being sawn in half, her back began to tingle.

Taking a deep breath, Claire whispered, "Lance, is that you?" There was a nearly inaudible scratching coming low on the door, as if from a small animal, followed by a light thud. She dropped the paper she was holding. It cascaded down slowly, landing with the words "only one way to stop" prominently showing. "Lance, you can come in now." Her heart was beating too rapidly. It felt like it had traveled up her bloodstream into her eardrums. "If you are still there."

She bit her lower lip, hard enough to draw blood. Trying to calm herself, she breathed deeply as a cloud passed over the moon, bringing darkness to the small space. Her fingers began to tremble and felt slightly numb. Frantically, she unraveled the bandana. Staring at her finger, she saw the flesh had turned to wood. The skin beneath it was wrinkled as if the blood had been drained, reminding her of the dead body beside her.

The door handle made a slight clicking noise as it slowly began to spin.

"Lance, if that's you, please say something!" There was no response. The only sound came from her own heartbeat and the wind. "This isn't funny!"

At the crack at the bottom of the door, she thought she saw the outline of a tiny foot in the shadow. Quickly, she went back to the wooden machine, frantically working the dials looking for the final instruction, hoping it would help explain whatever was happening. After aligning the shapes, the last piece of paper appeared, slowly ejecting from the side. Suddenly, the machine made a loud cracking noise, and the paper got stuck as it made its way out of the slot.

Claire tugged frantically, despite the cold sweat beading on her face. The paper wouldn't budge even an inch. She tried spinning the gears, digging her fingertips into the coarse wood, but it was as if they were glued down. Anxiety overtook her, making her slightly dizzy. Lifting the corner of the paper, she tilted it so she could read it in the moonlight. "To stop your companion, read this incantation aloud..."

The wooden case hid the next line. Hitting the top of the case repeatedly with her fists, the wheels remained stuck in place. Feeling like her heart was trying to beat itself out of her chest, Claire frantically pulled at the paper, tearing it as she heard the door creak slowly open, and the tiny footsteps of the forever wooden friend run quickly toward her.

Normal

by Justin Hunter

CHARLES WOKE. HIS OBLONG-SHAPED head rested on a thin pillow. He was looking toward the right, just as he always did. There was no real center to his body. The contractions took care of that. He liked to think that always looking off and to the right gave him a mysterious and aloof look. Mysterious and aloof sounded so much better than deformed. Women were never drawn to deformity unless they were those empathetic types who brought pity, sympathy, and a litany of never-ending inspiration-porn phraseology. Charles had no time for those. What were they to him? He was a grown man, and nothing felt worse than a woman the same age as him speaking to him like he was an infant. He would have liked to be able to take those women in strong arms and feel them melt into his embrace. He wanted to feel like a woman would want him for something other than to make themselves feel better.

He also wanted to know why he was facing the wall. Who put him this way?

Charles turned his head to the left as far as he could, which brought him to just beyond midline. He inwardly cursed his useless right arm as it hung limp from his shoulder, acting as a weight and holding him from going any further. The ventilator tubing tugged at his throat, and for a moment he did not move. Dislodging the trach from the ventilator would be a crap way to start the day. A quiet moment cut by the sounds of alarms. People running into the room and fussing over him. Waking in the morning was one of his life's small joys. He was alone, and he was almost never alone. Charles lay back to the right, facing the wall. It was then that he felt the wetness at his middle. The feeding pump must have disconnected at the port. Ensure was pooling underneath him. Charles knew there was nothing he could do about it and just let it be.

The bed moved. Charles dipped slightly to the left as the ironically named *Freedom Bed* turned his body. No bedsores for Charles. Not with the Freedom Bed. Every hour or so, he was rotated like an egg in an incubator. Charles winced as he felt the pressure release from his right leg and go to the left. His hips were disconnected at the sockets. His knee and ankle joints contracted, so that he was always sitting like a mountain Yogi. The dipping of the bed made the room he was in easier to see. Charles' eyes landed on the photo of his parents he kept at his nightstand. He looked first at his father, who died three weeks ago, then at his mother, who was very much still alive. He looked at their smiles and saw they were fake for the camera. He wondered if he'd ever seen them smile for real.

He heard the clipped and heavy tread of footfalls and knew Dr. Brandt was here. He smelled the man's Stetson cologne and then saw his kind-yet-serious and neatly shaved visage enter his view. Dr. Brandt was a hear-smell-see person. He knew his mother was also there when he saw her stand next to the doctor. His mother, Hilda, was a see-smell-hear person. Charles found them to be the most frightening type of person because they would always seem to appear out of nowhere. After seeing his mother, he got a slight whiff of talcum powder. He never heard her footsteps. She wore slippers in the house.

"Hi, darling," Hilda said. She began stroking his hair into a more acceptable level of disarray.

Hello. Charles wasn't able to speak the greeting out loud, but he never seemed to be able to stop thinking in conversation when someone spoke to him. His words came from software hooked up through his laptop computer. A headset which read his eye gaze put letters down on a screen. Charles, and everyone else for that matter, found the process slow and tedious. However, it was something. It was communication. He would be able to say if a part of his body hurt or ask for something particular to watch on television. He couldn't set up the works himself though, and the device was gathering dust in the far corner of the room. He guessed that his communicating wasn't top of the agenda for his caregivers, as they rarely deemed it necessary to hook up the system.

"Hello, Charles," Dr. Brandt said. "It's been a long time. You look well."

"He's made a mess of himself," Hilda said, pushing Charles up by a hip and watching as the feeding formula dripped down the mattress.

I didn't actively do that.

"I'll just have the nurse clean him up when she gets in," Hilda said. "She should get here within the hour." Hilda shut off his feeding pump and put the tubing over the medical pole.

"Of course," Dr. Brandt said. "I don't usually make house calls."

"I know," Hilda said. "Thank you so much for coming out. I just wanted to talk about what we could do for Charles here. Since my husband passed, it has been much more difficult to care for him."

"As I remember, we had difficulty with his surgeries before. His skin didn't tolerate the orthopedic splinting necessary for recovery."

"I don't think that will be a problem now. He's not a child anymore and I've been researching options like the materials they use for diabetics. There have been many advancements over the years, and I think we should try."

"That's true," Dr. Brandt said. "But you would have to follow the outpatient procedures as described."

"I know. That was my husband's fault. He didn't like to see Charles uncomfortable, and he would quit the orthotics too early. If Charles has skin issues, I'm sure they will heal with care."

"So, what are your goals for Charles?"

"I want him to be more normal-looking," Hilda said. "I want him to be able to sit. I don't like having him in bed all day. Maybe a little something with the feet. It would be nice to have him be able to wear shoes. Moving him is a lot of trouble for me, and the nurse mentioned it once or twice."

"How so?"

"The arms. His arms are awkward to get into the Hoyer Lift. He's also almost a grown man. He's heavy." Hilda lifted Charles' arm and dropped it. It fell across his chest and lay limp. Dr. Brandt put it back in place across his side.

"Charles," Dr. Brandt said. "I'm going to move you a bit. Okay?" Charles gave a slight sideways nod.

What did she mean by my arms are heavy?

"Well, we can talk about the sitting," Dr. Brandt said. "That's something we can take care of. First, we have to deal with the hips, as they are dislocated. We can get him realigned, but the movement will be restricted."

"What does that mean?"

"A lot of what we have to do involves fusing the joints into place. If you want him sitting, he will be sitting permanently. He can still lay down; his legs will not be able to be extended."

"That's fine."

"Once the hips are in place, we'll work on the legs. We can cut some tendons to increase range of motion for his contractures, then place rods inside the legs to hold them into position. This is what we should probably do because of his skin issues regarding orthotics. If the orthotics don't do what they're supposed to, then the rods will make sure the surgery aftercare works."

How many surgeries is that going to be? Four?

Dr. Brandt picked up Charles' left foot. He ran two fingers along the instep and pushed back slightly on the toes. He took the heel in his hand and gave it a slight squeeze and rotation. Charles winced at the touch.

"Does that hurt?" Charles nodded. "I apologize." Dr. Brandt put the foot down and turned back to Hilda.

"The shoes are going to be another matter," he continued. "We would have to shave the foot and shape it in order to make any type of shoe work. The foot is contracted inward and also curves up like an angry cat."

"Shoes would make him look so much more appropriate in public," Hilda said.

When in God's name am I ever in public?

"Don't worry," Dr. Brandt said. "It can be done. Now the arms."

"They really do get in the way."

***

Charles woke in his bed, rotating his body. His right side tilted upward. His shoulder pushed into the folding crevice of the bed, and he felt like he was going to fall. The warmth of his hand on his leg is no longer there. It's always after realizing the warmth is missing that

Charles remembers his hand is missing. As is his arm, all the way up to the shoulder. The other is gone as well.

Then the pain. It's his feet.

Charles shoved his upper body forward, thrusting his misshapen head down the tilted mattress until his chin rested on his right collarbone. He eyed his feet. They lay stacked, caged, and stabbed like one of those Cenobites from the movie *Hellraiser*. At least, that's how they looked to him. Some pins to hold them long. Some to hold them wide. Some pins to keep them straight. "A month of this," said Hilda, "and they'll look almost normal."

Horseshit, these will never look normal.

Charles tried to move his feet, but they might as well be under millstones. He figured they would become that normal shape—the type that fits into a shoe—but they were gouged and shredded. He was trading soft skin over a bent appendage for violation and straightness. This was normal? He used to have arms. Useless and hanging, but they were there. Was having no arms better? It was lighter for sure. Saved the nurse a few pounds of lifting.

Lopped them off like the dead branches of a tree. Here since my dawn and now gone. Can't put them back after taking them off. No way. No how. No dice, pal. I'm looking rather trim. I'm looking rather TRIMMED. Ha Ha!

Charles pulled his shoulder back, jerking his head back to its usual bend. His teeth ground. The pain pulsated up from his feet to his lower back, up his spine, and to the base of his skull. He began counting the pain throbs and flowing with the wash of sensation from bottom to top. He wondered when the nurse would come in with some pain meds. His gaze went to his word board, which was still sitting in the same place across the room. Spotless from dusting, not from use. His words.

My words.

He would ask for pain medicine.

I would ask for pain medicine.

"Hello, Charles," Dr. Brandt said. Charles' eyes darted to him, but the rest of his body did not move. "I hope I didn't startle you."

I used to be able to hear you coming. My ears worked fine. I wonder why I can't anymore. Maybe I'm preoccupied.

"How are you feeling?"

Poorly.

Dr. Brandt ran his fingers over the metal rods which pierce Charles' feet. He tightened one here. Loosened another one there. Charles grunted, and Brandt looked up. His eyes filled with compassion, and he picked up a file that sat on a small table next to the bed.

"I'm going to up your morphine," Dr. Brandt said. "I can't do it too much more than it already is, but we can do some." He made a few notes in the file and put it back down. He pulled a chair over next to Charles and sat, hands clasped and leaning forward.

"The feet are coming along nicely. Two more weeks until we can remove the pins. Sorry, you have to put up with them for a bit longer. The structure of the foot was only important as it pertained to getting it safely into a shoe. We didn't worry about much else except the shape since your feet weren't functional anyway. I've never had a surgery where I could just cut and shape. Working with you is like working with clay. There's an old joke that says if you want to make an elephant from a block of clay just remove anything that doesn't look like an elephant. To make this," he gestured to Charles' feet, "I just removed anything that didn't look like a foot. It's easier than you'd think. People don't know that with just a few cuts you can pull the foot flesh right off from the skeleton. People are walking around basically in flesh socks, they just don't know it."

Dr. Brandt touched Charles' left shoulder. Charles continued watching him.

"The arms were much more difficult. You can't just lop..."

Did he just say lop?

"...off an arm and burn the stump like in those horror movies. There's much more to that. Big arteries. You have to have skill."

Like those Civil War surgeons had to have skill. Piles of arms. Piles of feet.

"I wanted to let you know that there's going to be more."

Hilda.

"The shape of your skull, the way your neck tendon pulls your head to one side..."

No arms is better than useless ones?

"...we can re-cut that tendon and free your neck..."

Massacred foot-shaped things that fit into leather loafers.

"...you'll become cross-eyed if you keep your head like that. So we fuse the spine..."

I just want my words.

"...braces the neck to hold the skull. Add a rod to assist with the weight..."

I am a man. I am not made of clay.

"...we can cut the skull and then rebuild for the correct shape..."

Cut away everything that doesn't look like me. Then I'm a human.

Dr. Brandt pushed his thumb into Charles' thigh and then lifted it up. He gazed at the white spot left by his thumb on the skin as it quickly vanished.

"This might be a little off topic," Dr. Brandt said, "but I just thought about my butcher recently telling me to stick my thumb in the center of my burgers before cooking them. It keeps them from going round at the middle while they cook. Round burgers make it too tempting to press them with the spatula. Don't press them. It gets rid of all the good stuff. Keep them juicy."

I am meat. I am clay.

"No matter how much I try to stop myself," Dr. Brandt said, "I just can't stop myself from pressing them. I press."

And I am the mold.

Wire and Flesh

by M.J. McClymont

Elspeth inspected the damage the fall had inflicted on her knee. Pain had been a stranger to her for more years than she could remember, and even now she felt only concern for broken wire and torn moss. She glanced back accusingly at the rock she had tripped over and shook her head in frustration. She stood, flexing her leg and, when she was certain that the injury was not serious, took a tentative step forward.

The view from Beinn Bhán never failed to take her breath away, and it had brought her back time and time again. She returned so often, in fact, that the ascent had become part of her daily routine. She resolved to continue the trek until old age froze her joints and made her body too brittle to move, just like her sister, Morag, who had, in a prior life, claimed to have once met Robert Louis Stevenson on the streets of Edinburgh.

Up there on the apex, amongst the clouds, Elspeth felt at one with the land. Browns and greens of every variance sprawled out before her for miles into the hazy distance. The surface of the loch, framed by trees, would mirror the sky on a calm day, but today the tempestuous weather caused it to tantrum and churn fitfully. Elspeth could not feel the cold but shivered anyway; she felt it was only polite in the presence of such a wind.

On previous visits, when she had lain on the ground in that one special place she truly felt she belonged, her form had been indiscernible from rock, strata, and moss; not lost in the landscape, but part of it, at one with the mountain. She wondered how many others had stood there on the edge of the precipice, tall and defiant, enraptured by the beauty of the surrounding country. How many kindred souls had braved the ascent to be awarded this view? Had they developed the same affinity as she? Perhaps one day their paths would cross and a new chapter of Elspeth's life would commence. She could only hope.

She frowned at an ominous sky the shade of basalt, wondering vaguely if she would make it home before the downpour. As the thought faded, a fat, frigid droplet landed on her upturned face. Better to be on her way or she would be sodden for days.

The next blind step in her journey brought her further mischance when her foot slid on loose strata; she leaned back instinctively and went down hard on her rump. Decades old grit and mulch tumbled from the wound on her knee. Perhaps she would need some mending after all.

She reached the dookit just before midday, after a brief stop off at the old Campbell farm to procure first aid necessities. When she entered the gloom of the ramshackle hut, Morag and Nessa were sitting in their usual positions, completely inanimate, dark renderings of human forms, ashen outlines against a dark backdrop.

"Only me," Elspeth said, placing a length of coiled wire and a considerable square of mesh on the table between her sisters. She sat next to Nessa, clutching her knee.

"Up the Beinn Bhán again, oor Elspeth?" Nessa pressed her knuckles against her hips.

"Where else is there to go?"

"You better watch yersel', hen, it's only a matter of time before folk spot ye' striding it out around Applecross on yer tod. It's no safe out there on yer own."

"Ach, Nessa, there's naebody there to see me."

Nessa eyed the mesh and wire. "If you keep pilfering the farmers' fences, they'll soon come looking for answers. You mark my words..."

"Wheesht yer girnin'. Can you fix my knee or no?"

"Aye, and there's enough there to fix up the old one over there too."

Morag sat opposite, perfectly still. It was a skill she had honed out of necessity. She had remained in her current form far longer than she desired, at least four decades longer than Elspeth and three decades longer than Nessa. Skipping a generation had rendered her frail and misshapen. The network of rusted and corroding metal barely held the detritus of bracken and muck inside. A thick layer of moss had spread up her legs, creeping over her torso like filthy green leggings, and an unruly beard of wild grass sprouted from her chin.

Slowly, Morag shook her head. A shower of orange dust fell from her neck, littering the floor beneath. "No, sister. If I can't find a way to bring my youth back, then once this shell is gone, so am I. I'll be free of this form one way or another, but I won't be patched up like some idling automobile."

Elspeth sighed. The exchange had not been the first of its kind. Nessa and Morag bickered often but, fortunately, things had never grown sour between them over the centuries. They experienced the same misery in varying degrees. Even Elspeth longed for things most take for granted: the sensation of soft fabric on bare flesh, the taste of good food, the satisfaction of a warm bath on a winter's day. She suspected that the heady sensation of full-bodied red wine and the rich flavour of chocolate would be enough to send her hurtling into paroxysms of pleasure after so long without such luxuries.

Invoking the epicurean memories of those halcyon days of her past did little to mollify Elspeth. Like her sisters, her discontent was palpable. She hated being cooped up in the cramped, stuffy little box where she did not belong, where *they* did not belong. Every moment indoors was a moment squandered, a missed opportunity for a new lease on life. Sensing that it was not the time to voice her true feelings on the matter, Elspeth tried a different approach. "Your time will come, Morag," she said. "An opportunity will arise; it always has in the past, and it will again."

"Not many opportunities or anything else for that matter arising around here, Elspeth. This time it seems we've chosen the back of beyond, a stark contrast from our previous dwelling in the city. There were plenty of opportunities there; instead, we sit here, day in, day out, rotting away."

"Better that than being chased through the streets by pitchfork and torch mobs," Nessa snapped. "We almost didn't make it that time. Dae ye no remember eighteen seventeen?"

Elspeth needed no reminding; her mind was a trap for such experiences, and the memory made her shudder. "Walkers," she said, quickly changing the subject.

Morag and Nessa looked at her.

"Folk come from all over to hike up Beinn Bhán. I rarely see them over this end, but some o' them leave things behind at the top, crisp pokes and that."

"Yer joking, Elspeth!" Nessa threw her hands in the air and let them fall, the rocks in her wrists striking the table with the force of a swung hammer. "How on earth do ye expect yer sister to get up there? She can hardly balance on those rusty pegs of hers these days, let alone shuffle her old frame up the face of a mountain."

Morag turned her head to look at Elspeth. Orange confetti fluttered to the floor. "Nessa is right, hen; the tatties are o'wer the side."

"No, they're no, they'll be roastin' in the oven while we heat oor bones in front of a blazing hearth soon, Morag, trust me."

"Yet we're still sitting here on oor arses, talkin' about it and no actin' on it," Nessa said. "So let's go out and find these walkers of yours before they make their ascent."

"In the pourin' rain and howlin' wind," added Morag sullenly.

"It always pourin' of rain and blowin' wind, Morag, but why do you care, ye'll no feel it."

Nessa patched Elspeth's knee with the mesh, expertly weaving it into the existing network with the thick wire she had torn from the farmer's fence. When she was done, she began working on Morag, fixing the worst of the age-related wear, an artist applying glue to a fractured sculpture.

Elspeth hoped Nessa's efforts would be enough to hold her sister together for a while. She found herself incapable of imagining a future without Morag. The concept of loss seemed alien to her now, but she had no doubt that she would grieve if that sad day ever arrived.

Nessa helped Morag out of her seat and aided her to the door. When her older sister emerged from the hut and stood, staring at the sky, tracing the outline of the mountains, it dawned on Elspeth that this was the first time Morag had been outdoors in some years. She drank the sights like a thirsty cat lapping at a dripping faucet. Suddenly, her head tilted to one side.

"A dog," she said, the vegetation on her chin swinging like strings of drool as she tilted her head farther in a bid to improve her auditory senses.

Elspeth listened intently. She could hear the wind buffer the roof of the dookit like some great huffing beast, and the syncopated patter of rain, adding a beat to nature's soundtrack. Then, a gruff peel of barks carried by the wind chimed in, followed by the baritone of a male voice and the euphonious tinkle of a woman voice, redolent of the cadence of a wind chime.

It had been so long since Elspeth heard the voices of anyone other than her sisters. That mere element of variety caused a ripple of excitement deep inside. She turned, waving her arms, palms up in a failed attempt to shepherd her sisters back into the dookit. They were not for moving. She had forgotten how nerve wracking the process could be, and she hoped that another voice would join the duet soon so that she and her sisters could continue their journey together.

As the chatter of voices drew nearer, the sisters knew they had little choice but to freeze and hope the owners of the mellifluous utterances would regard them as mere man-made effigies.

The dog was the first to arrive, veering round the corner with little grace, sniffing the wire and earthen curios with a moderate level of interest. When the dog reached Nessa, it cocked its leg and urinated on her.

"Ach," she hawked, momentarily forgetting her silent pretense.

The dog flinched and backed away, watching Nessa closely, nose twitching in the air.

As the voices drew nearer still, Elspeth could follow their conversation.

"I don't understand it," the woman said. "Why would anyone want to pinch a load of wire?"

Elspeth's stomach lurched. In her peripheral vision she saw Nessa's head move incrementally.

"Told ye'," Nessa whispered, eliciting a raucous peel of barks from the collie. The dog disappeared for a moment, and when it returned, it was accompanied by the farmer and his wife.

Mr. Campbell stumbled to a halt. He gazed at the three wire sculptures with an expression of confusion, and then he stepped back, pulling a slender device out of his pocket and taking a photograph. "I think the mystery has been solved, love."

The woman drew next to him, her eyes flitting from Elspeth to Nessa and from Nessa to Morag. "What on earth is this?"

"Someone's art project, by the look of it."

"Oh my, they stink!"

The farmer laughed. "This is the best use of stolen property I've ever seen. Come on, you have to admit that they're quite something."

"And they're creepy."

"So lifelike in their posture, almost as though they're stepping out for a wander."

"I wonder who the culprit is."

"Maybe they are."

"Oh, stop it, you'll give me nightmares."

Farmer Campbell laughed as he gazed through the rain at the surrounding mountains. "They certainly have some beautiful scenery to mull over."

The woman moved within reach and Elspeth bit back the urge to seize her and steal her life as easily as she had stolen the wire from her property. But she did not; there were only two of them and it wasn't her turn. Breaking the unspoken rule would be an unforgivable act, particularly if her older sister perished as a result of her selfishness. Of what little festering tissue remained within her metal casing, there was a heart, at least in spirit form. That metaphysical organ beat harder for her sisters than for any other being on earth, living or otherwise.

Unaware of the peril in her actions, and to Elspeth's relief, Mrs. Campbell blindly reached for Morag's shoulder while exchanging words with the farmer.

When contact was made, Morag's shell unraveled.

Coils of wire slid round the woman's arm, and tendrils encircled her throat. She remained unaware of the movement, gazing up at Beinn Bhán while chatting to her husband's back. Then, when the needle-thin shards quickly burrowed into her neck and face, she screamed.

The farmer turned and dashed toward his wife, veering too close to Nessa, who slammed her stone-weighted fist into his forehead in a flurry of dust and grit. He stumbled back and Nessa gripped him tight, strips of wire leaving her filthy, golem-like form and stabbing the man all over, tearing his clothes and puncturing his soft flesh. He screamed and tried to throw off the wires, leaping and shaking like an over-strung marionette worked by a puppeteer in the throes of a fit. Endless lengths of metal created countless entry points in his flesh, sinking deep. In seconds, he was drenched in blood, and his lungs filled the air with agonized gurgling screams, oaths and frenzied pleas for mercy quickly turned to pleas for an immediate end, a quick escape from the excruciating pain that lit every nerve in his body. Meanwhile, the collie ran circles around them, barking wildly in confusion. Were its masters playing some strange new game? Were they in danger?

Elspeth retreated to the outer wall of the dookit. Of course, she had taken hosts in the past along with her sisters, but she had never been a spectator to the process. It seemed surreal, visceral, shocking. She offered a silent prayer that the suffering would be over quickly for the sake of the poor couple who had merely gone in search of their missing property. Had Elspeth been of flesh, she would have vomited at the sight of the bloodbath before her.

She forced herself to observe the man. He staggered as a thousand metal worms writhed beneath his skin until his head pulsed, a mass of subcutaneous cables, threatening to burst at any given moment, promising to spill the contents of his skull upon the ground.

The last of Nessa's wire wriggled into the man's wounds, and the amorphous heap of accumulated dirt, moss, pebbles, and twigs collapsed to the ground, splitting open upon impact. A filthy skull emerged from the mass, the vestige of a prior life. Its jaw dislodged as it rolled on the ground, stopping at Elspeth's feet.

The man collapsed and lay prostrate on the ground, unmoving. A few feet away, his wife lay, her face a lifeless crimson mask, head propped upon a pillow of mouldering rock and bone-infused soil that had once been part of Morag.

Elspeth rested the back of her head against the timber wall of the dookit in relief. The nasty part was over. The dog continued to run rings around his owners, barking in an attempt to rouse them. The intermittent growls and raised hackles of the animal indicated that it no longer considered their inaction a game.

"Morag?" Elspeth stepped forward, but not close enough to make contact with Mrs. Campbell's corpse. If the wire mesh of her metal epidermis touched the soft flesh of her new form, she would be unable to stop the process, ejecting Morag from her host and killing her sister. That was a risk she was not prepared to take, so she stepped back again.

"Morag," Elspeth repeated, marginally louder this time. The corpse remained still, sightless eyes penetrating the grey heavens. Then, as though Prometheus had injected the blazing element into his creation, Mrs. Campbell blinked. But it was no longer Mrs. Campbell.

The rain continued in earnest, washing the glaze of sticky crimson off Morag's face, a face of flesh and bone, of muscle and expression, of skin and life.

"Hello, sister." Morag sat, gazing around her, wide eyed, as though receiving the gift of sight for the very first time. "The glen looks different through new eyes. My voice..."

"Yer voice sounds lovely, a sweet sound fitting of yer new form."

"Nessa?"

Nessa approached tentatively, all the time inspecting her rough, calloused hands. She rolled her wide shoulders and flexed her new muscles. "I've never been a man afore," she said, grinning. "I think I shall enjoy being a man for a while." She beat her chest, grunted, and then giggled like a giddy schoolgirl.

Morag gazed all around her and then she stopped to comfort the dog, which had since ceased its protests and was now at heel next to Nessa. She began to describe the sensation, excitedly urging Nessa to feel the collie's fur. She did, and they spent longer than necessary on the mundane act. When they had grown bored of discussing forgotten sensations, they faced their sister in solemn silence. Nothing more needed to be said; they had all been in the situation Elspeth now found herself. No words could soothe the disappointment.

Elspeth stood back at a safe distance from them. A profound feeling of fathomless melancholy gripped her like the locked jaws of a rabid animal, threatening to crush her. She accepted that it was her turn to remain behind. When they finally returned for her, having lived out their stolen lives, she would be the frail one.

She watched Morag, envious of the tear spilling from her beautiful, blue, human eye. Morag placed a finger against her cheek as the tear traced a wet trail down her face. She caught it and raised her finger before her to inspect the droplet as it clung to her fingertip, shivering almost imperceptibly.

Morag sniffed. "You keep an eye out for those walkers, hen, you hear me? The moment that opportunity arises, seize it."

"Aye, Morag, I will." The urge to embrace her sister was almost irresistible, but she knew that any contact now would end her sister's life—the current one, and the chance of all future lives.

Then they turned their backs on the dookit. Elspeth watched them walk hand in hand, with the dog frolicking around them, barking intermittently. When they melted from sight into the haze of rain, Elspeth began her ascent to the only place she truly felt she belonged.

Perhaps in half a century her sisters would return and find her there still, a perch for gulls, fused to her favorite spot, gazing into the fading distance. To Elspeth, this did not seem like such a terrible way to spend her time.

The Year of the Cruise

by Alan Bax

Robert and Daisy were the cutest couple ever. They were in their early thirties, both physically fit, always nice to everybody, and very easygoing people. The couple never fought and frequently finished each other's sentences. They were not only husband and wife, they were best friends. While the other spouses their age were popping out babies, raising families, and mending their white picket fences, the Carters worked hard and played hard, stowing away all their cash each year for their epic vacations, and this year was no different. It was the "Year of the Cruise," as the charming couple so playfully referred to it. They had been naming all their vacations each year in this way. There was the "Year of the Wild," where all their trips were required to include hiking, camping, or some other such outdoor experience. There was the "Beer Year," where they went to dozens of breweries. There was the "Year of the Vineyard," the "European Year," and the "Year of Horrors," where they frequented scary locations and haunted houses.

The adorable couple would celebrate their tenth wedding anniversary on a cruise ship floating out over the Pacific Ocean. The cruise had arrived at the port in Manila on a Sunday morning, and they had spent all day discovering the city. Now they were running late, and were more than a little drunk, rushing to get back before the 10:00 p.m. deadline when the ship would depart once again, cruising all night and heading to the port in Yokohama, Japan. They would spend most of the next day out at sea, but were hoping to dock in time to devour plates of sashimi for their anniversary dinner. But now, on the eve of their wedding anniversary, the lovebirds were stumbling along the streets of Manila in each other's arms, enjoying the wonderful strangeness of being somewhere other than Raleigh, North Carolina.

They were flirting and zigzagging down the sidewalk when Daisy spotted a blinking red sign above an old door. There was an open palm on the sign, with some letters in a language they couldn't understand above it.

"Oh, Bobby, I've always wanted to get my palm read," Daisy said with a thick Southern accent. Back home, their family and friends said they didn't have any accent, but on this trip it had quickly become apparent that they did, and it became even thicker when they were drunk. She was pointing at the blinking sign and giggling, playfully trying to pull her lover across the street by the arm.

Bobby reluctantly allowed himself to be pulled across the uneven road, protesting as he stumbled behind her. "Daisy, we're already late. If that ship leaves without us, we'll be fucked."

Daisy let go of him and hopped up onto the other sidewalk, leaving his arm in the middle of the street. She turned and faced him with her hands on her hips and a playful grin on her face. "Oh, you know that ship won't leave without us. We'd sue the bastards for everything they had if they just gave us ten minutes before they took off. Anyway, they always give us an extra hour or so before actually departing, and this shouldn't take more than ten minutes."

Bobby came onto the sidewalk and took her hand. "Alright, but we only have about ten minutes, then we've really got to run. They won't wait forever, and they'll leave our asses after a while."

They walked hand in hand underneath the blinking red palm and entered the shop. A bell rang somewhere in the back of the place. They stood nervously in the lobby area with a black curtain blocking off another room in the back. Suddenly, an old lady emerged from behind the curtain, wearing a purple dress with a pink scarf wrapped around her head. She stood with the curtain pulled aside and waved them in without saying a word.

The couple gave each other one last awkward glance before walking past her and through the black curtain. Inside, the strange woman motioned them to sit down at a glass table with a crystal ball placed in the middle of it. The metal fold-out chairs squeaked as they sat down and the old lady sat across. The palm reader reached under the table and produced a fifth of whisky. The couple laughed and swayed drunkenly at this crazy-looking woman in an ugly purple dress.

The woman took a large swig out of the bottle, put it below the table, and extended her hand for payment. The adorable couple looked at each other, not sure how much to pay. Then Daisy spotted the sign on the wall that said *$20*, and Bobby dug in his pocket and paid the palm reader. Satisfied, the fortune teller reached across the table and took Daisy's right hand.

She glared at it, through it, rubbing her thin fingers along the pit of the palm. Then she pulled her hands away quickly, reached under the table, and pulled out the whisky again. She took another big gulp and flashed a sardonic, toothless grin as she shook her head slowly back and forth with one eye closed.

"It don't look good," she muttered across the table. "Just like all the others from that ship that I've read today."

The couple looked at each other, confused, and Bobby had a question. "What does 'It don't look good' mean, exactly? Does that mean something bad is going to happen on that boat? Is it a shipwreck? Food poisoning? What's going to happen?"

The old woman shook her head with both eyes closed and pushed the twenty-dollar bill back to the couple. "No, it don't work that way. I don't predict the future. I just read the palms. It looks like something bad is going to happen to you soon, just like every other palm I've read today. It could be a hangover, for all I know. Now take your money and get out of my home. I'm done reading for today."

She took another swig of whisky and motioned her hand at them for the couple to leave. They got up and walked through the curtain, out the door, and onto the sidewalk. They didn't speak until they were halfway up the block, walking fast and holding hands.

"The good news is it didn't take very long. So, should we get on the boat?" asked Daisy.

Bobby stopped and put a hand on each of her shoulders, looking lovingly into her eyes. "Listen, I'm not letting some old lady ruin our 'Year of the Cruise,' are you?"

He saw her worried face turn into a large, mischievous grin. God, he loved this woman.

Daisy shook her head and felt the happiness coming back to her. "No. I guess not."

She put her arms around him and their lips met in the dimly lit streets of Manila. There was no one else on this side street, just the two happy lovers, drunk and embracing. They stumbled carelessly in each other's arms to the busier main street and, eventually, found their way to the cruise ship. They were over a half hour late and nobody seemed to notice.

That night, after drinking wine from the bottle and making love for over an hour, they went to sleep naked and sweaty in each other's arms. In between the lovemaking and the sleep, they joked about the soothsayer's gloomy prediction, but they were much too happy to take such pessimism seriously.

The next morning, they woke up too late for breakfast and went to eat lunch at the on-boat restaurant instead. They were hungover, but still in good spirits.

Daisy flipped through the menu. "I think I'm having a salad."

Bobby grabbed the menu, turned to the entrees page, and then declared, "I'm having the seared sea scallops and another beer."

He waved down a server and tapped the empty bottle. "Did you see that mime at the pool today? That guy was pretty freaking cool, wasn't he?"

"Did you just tap your beer? You know that's like snapping your fingers at her. It's rude."

Bobby smiled. "I'm sorry, honey. I know you want today to be special. Sorry about the sunburn too. I'll try to class it up a little from now on." He paused and took her hand, holding it in the middle of the table, next to the cheese sticks. "I can't believe it's been ten years."

He reached into his pocket with his free hand and pulled out a diamond ring, holding it up before sliding it on her finger. "Happy anniversary, I love you, honey."

Daisy reached across the table and took her lover's hands into hers. "Oh, Robert." She was fighting back the tears. "It's so beautiful, and unexpected. I didn't get you anything, except that stupid card. The trip was supposed to be it."

She let a tear come out and wiped it from her eyes with her shoulder. They squeezed each other's hands, and then Daisy composed herself.

"I can't believe it's been that long, either. I still love you, though; I love you so very much, Bobby. I hope you know that."

A perverted smile formed on Bobby's face. "You can prove it tonight."

"I think I proved it last night." Daisy giggled and pulled her hands away from his, wiping the last bit of tears from her face. She closed the menu, then gazed across the table at her husband. "Were you going to do this over sushi tonight?"

"Yeah, but since we're not going to make it to port in time, it kind of ruined my plans. I figured I'd just do it at lunch since we both hated dinner here the last time, and we would probably be eating pizza or something later anyway."

"Good call. Pizza for dinner sounds amazing."

The server brought the beer to the table and the couple continued to laugh and have a good time together. They celebrated their anniversary as the ship swayed back and forth, moving about by the sloshing of the dark waters beneath.

After lunch, the couple put on their bathing suits and set up two seats by the pool. They hung their towels over them and reclined in the blazing sun.

"Are you going to get your ciggies?" Bobby asked.

Daisy pulled a twenty from the bag. "Yeah. You need anything?"

"Can you get me a beer from the bar?"

Daisy was already walking away and turned her head to yell behind her. "No problem."

Daisy went into the small shop and looked around. There wasn't much, but she couldn't help it; she was on vacation and just wanted to buy something. Her eyes darted across the aisles, and she found herself in front of the toys, eyeing a Bikini Barbie doll. She picked it up, remembering her dolls she had as a little girl. Daisy used to have an entire collection of them until they burned up in the fire just after her tenth birthday. She remembered waking up to the smell of thick smoke, and seeing her father appear in the doorway before coming in and rescuing her, carrying her outside the house where she could breathe again. There were the fire trucks and firefighters running around, splashing water on the house as it fell and burnt to the ground. A soggy, steamy ash was all that remained when the morning came. She remembered walking through the destruction, finding the burnt severed head of one of her dolls, and carrying it with her, the last remnant of that collection. She still had the burnt doll head at her house, one of the few keepsakes she kept from her childhood. Daisy seemed to recall having a Barbie doll that looked just like this one in her collection. Feeling a little silly, she bought it.

The girl behind the counter was in her early twenties and in a revealing little bikini. She was petite and beautiful, but she had dark circles underneath her eyes. Daisy thought it was probably from partying too hard the night before.

"Can I help you?" the girl asked.

"Yeah, I'll take a pack of Marlboro Lights."

She finished at the counter, and on her way to the bar, she passed by a group of five or six children that sat listening to an old man speak. The old man had a shirt on that said "Tales of the Deep" and he was spinning some yarn about shipwrecks and sea creatures. She stopped to listen for a moment. The old man's face was sallow and sickly, and he was speaking ominously in order to appropriately scare the children. He was also very drunk.

"It was one of those huge ones that had all kinds of entertainment; there was an entire circus on board when it went down. The survivors spoke of seeing enormous elephants drowning in the ocean, and there was a giant tiger that survived floating on the debris. Many of them swore it was the ghost ship that did it. There's a lot of speculation about what they really are. Some say that they're dead sailors, like from that other story. But others claim they aren't ghosts at all, but some type of creatures from beneath the ocean. There are mysteries we may never find out, children, and then there are some discoveries that we may live to regret. However, we don't know whether they're ghosts or not. They could be little green men for all we know." The man coughed violently and finished whatever was in his paper cup before resuming, with his eyes half closed. "And if we don't know of them, then maybe they aren't aware of us. Perhaps, to them we are the ghosts, or wavy, otherworldly creatures seen hovering over them when they venture just far enough from home. Anyway, that's the story, children, the story of the ghost ship full of..."

Daisy stopped listening to the old man and looked at the watching children, noticing that many of them had dark circles under their eyes and appeared sickly. They couldn't have all been drinking too much last night, could they? She hurried to the bar to get the drinks and head back to the pool. The bartender was a young, muscular man with a dark tanned chest, but he leaned against the bar as if he was worn out, and he kept sniffling and wiping his nose.

"What you want?" he said, and then coughed violently, bent over with both hands on his knees. They were deep, purposeful coughs, like he was trying to cough something up from somewhere deep down inside. He came up and snorted the remaining snot out of sight. "Sorry about that. I guess I'm a little sick. What'll it be?"

"Two beers?" she asked with a look of disgust.

He pointed at her, trying to play off the coughing fit. "Two beers, coming right up." He grabbed two cans. She snatched them away and was happy to be heading back to the pool.

She sat down by her husband and handed him a beer. "I noticed lots of people looking hungover today. They've got dark circles under their eyes, and the bartender was coughing up a lung."

"Maybe they're sick. We need to be careful. You know these cruises get outbreaks of viruses and stuff all the time. How are you feeling?"

"I'm feeling fine. You?"

He shrugged. "Good, so far."

Daisy reclined in her chair. "Well, I guess we can just take some extra vitamin C when we get back to the room." She took a deep breath and thought of home. "I wonder if Checkers is alright. I think I'll call Mom later and see how he's doing. We've never been away from him for this long, and cats are finicky little bastards, you know?"

Bobby didn't answer. Instead, he just gave her the thumbs-up sign, signaling that he was already in relaxed mode. When Bobby was in relaxed mode, he would just sit there staring through his sunglasses and, every once in a while, as if to prove he was not asleep to anyone watching, he would lift his beer and take a drink.

After five or six cans of beer, the couple went back to their room. They had planned on getting dressed and going to eat some pizza in the restaurant, but they both had dark circles under their eyes and didn't feel too good, so they decided to go to bed early. Bobby went to sleep immediately, with the lights still on, just after seven. Before she turned the lights off and joined him, Daisy pulled out the Barbie. It had on a skimpy bikini, and was staring back at her wide-eyed and open-mouthed through the clear plastic box that surrounded it. She took the doll out of the package and got under the covers, rolling over on her side and holding it close to her chest, like she had done long ago before the fire.

That night, Daisy had a horrible nightmare and woke up in a cold sweat, clutching the doll in her hands. In her dream, she was trapped inside the Barbie doll. She could peer out the eyes of the doll, but couldn't move the plastic body. She just lay on the floor of a toy store, face down and removed from the protective box. She tried to scream, but couldn't get the doll to make a sound, the screaming only going on inside of her. When Daisy awoke, the sheets were dripping wet and her face was wrinkled and water-soaked from lying on the soggy pillow all night. She went into the bathroom and wiped the moisture off her face with a towel, then she flipped over the pillow and tried to go back to sleep for a little longer. It was just after midnight and Bobby was snoring loudly; so loudly that she was having trouble getting to sleep again. In between snores, she could swear she heard whispering in the hallway, but she was too tired to care, and soon Daisy was dreaming again.

It was just after ten in the morning when she woke to the sounds of Bobby vomiting. He was coughing violently, and his head was burning hot when she touched it. Daisy put on some black shorts and a white t-shirt and went out to grab him some cough medicine, Tylenol, and whatever else that store had. While she was walking to the shop, she noticed the boat was moving more violently than she remembered, rocking back and forth so much that she had to steady herself as she moved. There were very few people up and moving about, and when she got to the store, there was no medication left; it was all sold out. She grabbed one of the last bottled waters and walked to the register. The clerk behind the counter looked even sicker than the day before, barely able to stand upright.

"What's going on? Is everybody sick? Why's the ship moving so much?" Daisy asked.

The clerk rolled her eyes; this was not the first time she had been asked those questions. "Everyone is sick, there's, like, a nasty virus going around. That's why no one is having fun. As for the ship, I don't know why it's moving so much, could be that we're really far out in the ocean." She flashed a fake smile, and Daisy left the store.

She made it back to the room, and her stomach was grumbling. As the day went on, she got sicker and sicker. They ate the fruit and chips they had in the room, since they were too weak to go out in public. That night, she began puking and cursing the cruise.

Throughout the night, the couple was in and out of the bathroom, barely staying hydrated, as they emptied their bodies of sickness. They found some aspirin and vitamin C that Daisy had brought with her and took them liberally. They were dizzy; the room was spinning, and the two of them were in and out of consciousness until the sun came up the next day. When the couple awoke at just after six in the morning, they were feeling slightly better, and starving. They went out together to see about getting something to eat.

The entire ship was a mess. There was trash strewn through the hallways, and all the restaurants and stores were locked up. The pool was full of trash and puke. The stench on the ship was unbearable. They saw no one else while exploring the boat, and there were signs of riotous behavior from the night before.

They were both scared, but it was really early, and it was possible that everyone may just be sick and still in bed. They decided not to panic yet, and to just head back to their room and come back out later on that morning. As they reached the hallway leading to their room, an elderly couple appeared, eyeing them suspiciously.

Daisy waved them down frantically, jogging toward them as she yelled. "Hey! We're the Carters. How are you? Do you know what's going on around here?"

The old man looked at the old woman, then both of them turned toward Daisy with tired eyes. The elderly man spoke in a quiet, hushed voice. "Please, keep your voice down. You don't want them to hear you. I suggest that both of you be as quiet as possible and just go back to your room for now."

They turned to leave, and Daisy grabbed the woman's arm, turning her around as she begged the couple, "Please, please tell us what's going on. We're both very sick and something strange is happening on this ship. If you know anything, please tell us. We have a right to know!"

The old man pulled a kitchen knife out of his pants and glared at Daisy's arm. She pulled it away as Bobby came up behind her to diffuse the situation.

"Hey, we're just scared now. There's no reason for any problems here," Bobby told the stranger. "Do you know what's going on or not?"

The old man's eyes were cold as glaciers, and he kept the knife raised as he spoke. "The whole boat is sick. Last night there was a mutiny or something, and they threw the captain overboard. They've all gone insane. Maybe it was the sickness, but whatever it was they were forming small groups together and they were all going around beating up and harassing random people. We saw them raping a woman, a child really, while the others were throwing people off the ship, all in the name of fun, just laughing and having a good old time as they did it. There's a big group of them that have gone insane, or maybe were insane the entire time and planned the whole thing, I don't know. What I do know is that you should try to hide somewhere as quickly as possible. We're going to find a hiding place now. The rooms aren't entirely safe. They came around knocking on doors last night, and they'll break them down eventually. Plus, we've got no food in our room. No one's operating the boat. We're floating out in the ocean and not going anywhere right now. I suggest you be prepared to defend yourselves and find some food. Good luck to the both of you." The old man backed away with knife raised, holding his wife by the arm, and they disappeared around the corner of the long hallway.

Daisy and Bobby stood frozen in panic. Then they heard loud, drunken voices from somewhere, and they rushed back to their room to come up with a plan. They looked around for any weapons they could use. Daisy found a pen and put it in her pocket. Bobby was sweating, sitting on the bed and holding his head. Daisy stood up and grabbed the wooden chair she had been sitting on. She broke the legs off against the floor, grabbing one of the splintered legs and handing the other to her husband. He was getting sicker, but he took it, coughed violently, and then stood up from the bed and nodded that he was ready to go.

Daisy kissed him hard on the mouth and pulled back, hands on his arms, and mouthed "I LOVE YOU." He mouthed back "I LOVE YOU TOO." The cute couple slowly opened the door and crept into the hallway, carefully moving through the boat to find food and shelter. They tiptoed down the halls, through the tunnels of the ship, hearing nothing but the ocean crashing all around them. They reached the end of a hallway and approached the entrance to the pool area where they had been reclining on their anniversary. Daisy peered around the corner to see a group of five men beating up a young boy and girl, each no older than twelve, taunting them as they kicked and punched the kids on the other side of the pool. Daisy led her husband behind the bar that was a few feet in front of them.

They stayed hidden there for hours, Bobby trying not to cough, and Daisy clutching a fifth of vodka that she'd almost finished. It had finally gotten quiet by the pool, and Daisy peeked her head over the bar and saw that no one was there. She squatted next to Bobby, who was pale as a ghost.

"Bobby," she whispered, trying to hold back the tears, trying to be strong enough for both of them. "I'm going to go look and see what's going on real quick. I need you to stay put, stay right here, and don't cough. You need to stay as quiet as you can and keep holding that wooden leg. Understand?"

Bobby nodded, breathing hard. "Yeah. I'll stay put. You just be careful."

Daisy kissed his forehead, and she knew his fever was well over a hundred, but she had to do something. She had to find out more about what was going on. She put down the vodka bottle, held tightly to the wooden leg, and rushed out from behind the bar with her back hunched over. She moved all the way to the side of the boat and looked out over the ocean.

The sun was bright and shining on dozens of bodies floating in the water. Some were still alive, flailing about, while others were motionless. She stood in awe of the scene before her for a few moments, then turned to see if anyone was around. Daisy could see three dead bodies on the other side of the pool, but no other living person. She looked across the pool for a weapon, but saw none, and figured she would have to make do with the liquor bottles. She scuttled back behind the bar and took another gulp of vodka. Then she heard the voices of men coming closer from the other side of the pool area. She listened to them carefully from behind the bar, trying to learn what she could about what was going on.

"Get over here, wench," one of the drunk men yelled. "Rick, you throw her over."

There was the sound of struggling, possibly feet kicking the side of the boat, and then a grunt. Daisy thought she could hear a faint splash, but wasn't sure. She held Bobby tightly. Then, out of the corner of her eye, she glimpsed something move past the bar, a shadowy thing. She turned, and it wasn't there anymore. Before turning back, something else caught her eye.

She thought she could see a hand appearing over the side of the boat on that side. She let go of her husband and he dropped to the ground. Daisy put her hands on either side of her face and opened her mouth wide in horror at what she saw, but no sound came out. She could not scream.

A figure pulled itself onto the boat with that hand she had seen. Then four more figures pulled themselves onto the ship, none of them seeming to notice her with her mouth wide open. She heard the sounds of the drunken men stop as she stared in horror at the side of the boat where the figures had been. The first one had a skeletal face; no, it *was* a skeleton, with tattered old clothes hanging off it that were drenched with the ocean. The second one was wearing a clown suit and a pirate hat. The other three were nothing but bones with a patchwork of rotting flesh still intact, and they moved quickly as they passed out of sight in front of the bar.

From behind the bar, Daisy could hear screams, the sound of ripping flesh, the thump of body parts falling onto wood, and then there were no more screams; there was no sound at all except for the creak of the ship, the waves crashing, and the sloshing and dragging of wet things across the wooden boards. Daisy's mouth was still open, but when she saw the skeletal face peek out from around the side of the bar and stare at her through the eyeholes of the skull, she shut her mouth, bit her lip, and lifted the wooden leg, but she could not swing it downward onto the ghastly thing. Daisy looked up and saw the clown in the pirate hat holding the piece of wood and preventing her attack.

It was unreal how strong the clown thing was as it pulled the weapon out of her numb hands. Then the other skeletal-faced thing put five bony fingers around her arm and dragged her body along the floor, around the bar, and out into the open. As she moved across the floor, her face turned back to see another evil thing dragging her husband by the arm and leading him to a place beside her.

The clown and the skeletal-faced creature stood watching the cute couple while the other two monsters kicked the body parts of their victims into the water. Then they went to the side of the boat and waved for others to come aboard. Daisy's head whirled as all manner of creatures came onto the ship, from all sides.

There were more clowns, and little people not even four feet in height, although they couldn't really be called people at all. What once was a man was now a legless stump that used its arms to pull its torso onto the boat and across the deck. A giant body, standing almost eight feet tall, was one of the last to pull itself on board. Then, right in front of them, what was once a bearded lady in a long, white dress crawled over the side and staggered past them to join a group of clown pirates.

It was an entire circus, a freak show of the dead. There were maggots crawling out of their skulls, and the wrinkly, water-soaked, patchwork skin looked like it could slide off the bones at any moment, as if they had been submerged in water for years, centuries even. They barely seemed to notice the couple at first as they gathered around the pool. Then the bearded lady pointed in their direction, and the things moved toward them. Her husband was on the ground with his eyes closed, unconscious from the fever or the shock. One of the creatures dragged Daisy toward the side of the boat, leaving Bobby on the ground behind her. It held her down as the others ventured down the hallways and into the further recesses of the cruise ship.

It was well after dark when they stopped searching. When one of them found a passenger, they would bring them out and nonchalantly throw them over the side of the ship. Daisy just sat and watched as they did this over and over again. Bobby would occasionally move around on the floor, but he never opened his eyes or seemed to wake up from his sickened daze. By the time the sun was going down in the sky, all the creatures were back by the pool. It seemed that the entire ship had been cleared, except for the married couple.

Finally awake, Bobby pulled himself up onto his knees. It took all his energy just to keep his head raised in order to maintain eye contact with his wife at the side of the boat. Daisy wept with the zombie gripping her head, holding it firmly in place. Something was about to happen and they both knew it. They could feel it. All the creatures stood and watched, all of them grinning as the human spoke to her husband for the last time, with tears pouring from her eyes.

"This has been the most wonderful ten years of my life. I love you so much, honey. You fight them, you hear me? You get out of here and you survive!" The creature grunted, and with one arm it lifted her up by the head and squeezed. Her eyeballs bulged and blood spurted out of her ears. Then it dumped Daisy over the side of the boat.

Bobby thrust his arm out and let out a muffled, bellowing moan. Then he fell to the ground and cried. The creatures ignored him, except for one clown who stood watch over him as he wept. Finally, the crying turned to laughter, and then to madness. Bobby Carter's eyes grew tired, things got dizzy all around him, the world spinning out of control, and then he passed out.

While the human went to sleep, the creatures went to work. The sun went down, and in the darkness of night, the cruise ship changed direction and headed east.

***

The boat was gone now, and it was so dark that Daisy's body could barely be seen floating on the surface of the ocean, moving peacefully back and forth, not even noticing when the translucent tentacle formed itself around her ankle and pulled her below the surface. The tentacle was thin and wiry, but strong, and it pulled her deeper and deeper into the depths of the sea. As her body went deeper, the pressure of the water increased; and when her body was almost swallowed up by the darkness, that was when her eyeballs popped out and lazily floated upward, away from her rapidly descending body.

She descended farther and farther. Her cheeks tightened against the skull, and then her jaw crumpled and became misshapen as the tiny bones in her face were being crushed. Her body was surrounded by darkness now, both above and below.

Suddenly, thousands of tentacles rushed upward as her body rushed downward, forming around what was once Daisy, congealing into a type of shield around her body, then pulling her down at a much faster speed. The body sped into depths that would easily snap the thickest human bones and normally flatten the human body, but Daisy's body stayed intact inside the cage of tentacles. A large, glowing animal with razor-sharp teeth gazed in alarm as this human body rushed past it into the deepest parts of the sea. The predator watched as the body disappeared into a trench in the ocean floor, and only a clustering of bubbles escaped and floated upward out of the hole. The glowing thing turned and swam away, lighting up the darkness as it searched for its next meal.

In the very depths of the Pacific Ocean, thousands of feet below the glowing predator, in an ocean within the ocean, the water flowed upward, and there was light everywhere. Deep within an underwater cave was a floating laboratory where two things floated in front of a clear substance, similar to glass, through which they were watching an empty room with three dark walls.

The companions were scientists, just like all the ten thousand or so other creatures in this underwater laboratory. At these depths, they were only about ten feet tall and over twenty feet wide. Everything inside of their bodies was completely collapsible upon itself, and they had no bones that would break at the intense pressures that existed this far beneath the sea. Their bodies were made of a cartilage-like substance that was unknown to humans, and it made them almost completely malleable. Their skin was scaly, and the ends of their appendages were razor sharp. The pressures at these depths forced their shape, and although their kind had not walked on land for millions of years, when they had ventured into the upper ocean where the pressure was minimal, they were as tall as fifty feet, and about twenty feet in width. They had two legs and two arms, much like humans, and when they weren't floating, they could walk like any other bipedal animal. Their V-shaped heads were almost entirely covered with two large yellow eyes. They had no mouth, since it was unnecessary for speech or for food intake. They were telepathic beings, and in the deep ocean water there were little microscopic organisms that floated everywhere, and the scientists would just open the pores on their skin to let the ocean water enter inside, and these tiny organisms would provide their sustenance.

The two things in the cave floated in front of the transparent wall and waited. They spoke to one another through nonverbal messages sent from inside one mind to the other.

Is it almost done?

Almost.

How is the exploration?

They have a ship and the Elder Minds are controlling them right now. We think they should make it much longer than the last ones.

That is good. Praise Thing.

Praise Thing.

The body of Daisy Carter descended into the empty room and floated within the protective tentacle bubble. The two things studied her intently as they spoke.

Her eyes came out like the others'.

Yes, we really must get to them sooner.

No matter, the Elder Minds do not need eyes to see. Ready?

They floated out of the cave and down onto the rocky floor beneath. There were large holes in the ground, and there were things floating in and out of them as the two walked across the bottom of the ocean trench. They walked in silence toward one of the holes and fell into it feet-first.

The hole was deep, and the two floated side by side for several minutes before coming to rest in a type of hallway. They walked to the end and entered a large, dimly lit room filled with twelve things that looked just like them that were seated on the ground, eyes closed, in a state of deep meditation.

The two scientists stood and watched the meditating things for several minutes. Then they turned and walked back down the hallway and floated up the hole. When they were out of the hole and walking along the rocky floor heading back to the cave, one of them stopped and turned to the other.

Did you see it?

Yes. I saw off the side of the ship. I saw the high-above place. Then I looked up and there were lights above that.

Those are separate worlds high above the separate world up there. Our ancestors came from those lights above that. They settled up where the explorers are now, long ago, before coming below.

I understand. Will this explorer be with the next group?

No. The Elder Minds are using her for a much longer experiment.

Suddenly, there was a rumbling under their feet, beneath the rocky floor. It grew louder and louder as the ground shook violently and the water vibrated everywhere. It was some type of underwater earthquake, and it sent all the things swimming quickly out of their holes and upward, away from the floor.

There was a roar from somewhere far below this place as the quaking stopped, and everything was peaceful and still once again. Everything went back into their holes again, and the walking and floating commenced. The two scientists descended back down to the ocean floor and faced each other, tipping their heads downward in a partial bowing motion.

Praise Thing.

Yes. Praise Thing.

They walked and then floated into the cave, to their laboratory, to study the body of Daisy Carter.

***

When Robert Carter awoke, he was barely feeling sick at all, just a little groggy and worn out. He was in their room on the ship, lying in bed. Where was Daisy? Had it all been a dream? He had been really sick and could have imagined the whole nightmare on the ship. Then the doorknob turned and in waddled the four-foot-tall creature with the fleshless face.

It was no dream; Daisy was dead. His heartbeat fluttered, beating way too fast for normal, and the room was spinning. A little wet hand pressed against his chest and he lay back down as someone, or something, put the covers over his chest. When he opened his eyes, he saw the door closing and the room was empty once again.

He sat up, fighting back the disorientation, and saw two open cans of tuna fish on the table next to two white pills. What was going on? Why hadn't they just killed him? Bobby rushed to the door, but it was locked. Daisy was dead. He fell to his knees and sobbed, wiping his tears away with a forearm. He wanted to eat the tuna, but a sudden rush of guilt caused the tears to flow even harder. How could he be thinking about eating when Daisy was dead? The crying stopped again, and his eye caught the tuna. His stomach twisted, he winced, and then he grabbed the can and scooped out the tuna with his fingers.

After he had eaten, he put the pills under the mattress. They looked like Tylenol, but he couldn't be sure. Whatever these things were, he remembered what his wife had told him, and decided that he was going to survive. He would do it for Daisy.

Suddenly, a phone rang somewhere in one of his suitcases. It was his cell phone!

On the screen it said HARVEY, his younger brother. He answered the phone quickly.

"Harvey! Harvey, you've got to call the police or FBI or something. They've taken over the ship and—"

Harvey interrupted him. "I know all about it, Bobby. It's all over the news. They're coming for you, they're coming for all of you. The military's going to kill those fucking pirate bastards. They're going in right now to get you. It's all over the news and everything."

"Harvey!"

But the phone beeped, and the screen went black. The phone was dead.

From somewhere outside the room, he heard gunshots. Then the entire room rocked as an explosion rocked the ship, sending him flying across the room. His head collided with the corner of the bed, and everything went black.

***

Harvey Carter was the first face that Robert saw when he awoke inside the largest hospital in Raleigh, North Carolina. His little brother smiled down at him, and Bobby spoke for the first time in he didn't know how long.

"Where am I?"

"You're in the hospital and you've been in some coma-type thing for about two days." Harvey placed an index finger to his skull. "You banged your noggin, but the doctors say you'll be all right. It was that virus that almost killed you, that and the dehydration."

Bobby sat up in the bed, holding his head and realizing for the first time just how many tubes were stuck in his arms. A nurse came rushing through the door and went straight to checking the machines. She was young, cute, and fresh out of college. The nurse stopped checking the equipment and put her hands on her hips.

"Well, it's about time you woke up, Mr. Carter," the nurse said in a thick Southern accent. "For a while there, we thought you wasn't gonna be walking out of here on your own anytime soon. We thought we might even have to wheel you out under the covers. Now, let me check you out." She checked his blood pressure and all the other things that nurses check before the doctor comes in.

"My brother told me I was out for two days?"

The nurse continued running her checks as she talked. "Kind of. You were unconscious when you came in here two days ago. You woke up for a little while after you arrived but were too weak to talk to anyone, so we kept the room closed for visitors. Then you've been in and out of sleep, resting and recovering, ever since. No coma though, and your brother's an idiot."

"Hey." Harvey looked insulted but then smiled playfully, touching her arm as if they had known each other for years. The nurse gave him a flirty glance and continued.

"Everything looks good." She finished checking his blood pressure and smiled reassuringly. "The doctor will be in any minute."

She was still smiling as she rushed out the door before he could ask any questions.

Bobby looked at his brother in disbelief. "Did I dream the whole thing? I mean, the zombies and Daisy, and the whole cruise?"

Harvey looked confused. "Zombies? What are you talking about?"

"You know, the entire cruise ship being taken over and everything. Is Daisy still alive?"

Harvey looked at the floor and back again. "Daisy's gone, brother. They're all gone. You didn't dream anything. This is as real as it gets. You were the only survivor, and they're going to be in here in a few minutes to tell you more. They call it debriefing in the movies, I think."

"Debriefing?" he muttered to himself. "But what about the—"

He was interrupted when the door flew open and a man in a dark suit closed it behind him. The man walked beside the bed and motioned for Harvey to leave. He did, waving innocently at his older brother as he left. The man in the dark suit waited until Harvey had closed the door behind him before he spoke.

"Mr. Carter, I am William Clinton. Yes, that is my real name, and you can call me Bill. Now, I'm sure you have a ton of questions, and I am here to answer them. However, before I do, I want to explain exactly what happened to you from the time of your abduction until you got to Raleigh. Do you need some water or anything?"

Robert shook his head and let the man continue.

"Good. Well, let's see. Three days ago, the cruise ship you were on got raided by pirates somewhere off the coast of an island just north of Guam."

"They weren't pirates, they were zombies. I know what I saw."

The man flashed a sardonic grin. "I don't care what you saw, Mr. Carter. May I finish?" He was still grinning, and Robert nodded in the affirmative. "Thank you. Now, these pirates took over the ship and killed everyone on board. From what we can tell, they threw most of the passengers overboard. Anyway, for some reason they kept you alive. Just you, and no one else." He stopped smiling. "Then they steered the ship to a tiny little island eastward where they killed many of the locals in the small village near where they landed. So we sent out our soldiers and they raided the island, killing every single one of those pirates, and very few civilians. Upon investigating the cruise ship, they found you, with a nasty bruise on that head of yours, and all covered in puke, but still alive. They flew you home, got you well, and here you are. Now, I'm sure you'll want to get a lawyer and sue that cruise ship for a ton of money. I don't care about all that. And there will be a funeral for your wife, God bless her soul. However, all I want to know is, when you leave here today, the press—and believe me, there will be a ton of press outside just waiting to talk to you — when the press asks you about the murderers that took over your ship, are you going to be a liar and call them zombies, or are you going to tell the truth and call them what they were?" He leaned in close. "Pirates. What are you going to say, Bobby? I need to hear it from you before I can let you leave this hospital." He flashed that shit-eating grin again, and Bobby sighed. He was tired.

"I'm going to say pirates."

The man stuck out his hand, and Bobby shook it. Then the man leaned back, surveyed the room, and took a deep breath with his chest stuck out.

"You're going to be a rich man, Bobby. Just do not lie to the press and you can go on with your life as best you can. I really am sorry about your wife, Daisy." He looked down at Bobby, looking into his eyes. "I truly am sorry for your loss, Mr. Carter. We lost a lot of people on that cruise ship, including Daisy, and you can believe me when I say that your government is looking for the source of those evil pirates as we speak. If there are any more of them above or down below the water, we will not rest until they are dead." He leaned in closer. "We will go down and drag the fuckers out of the ocean one by one if we have to. They will pay for what they've done. I promise you that, Bobby." He nodded to the patient and walked away, carefully closing the door behind him.

Harvey came back in, and Bobby eventually got better and went home. He went back to his empty house and Harvey stayed with him for two months, through the funerals and the interviews in the press, but eventually he had to go back to work, and Bobby was alone. With the money he got from the life insurance, combined with the settlement he was getting from the cruise line, he decided to quit his job. Robert Carter would never have to work again. He was a very rich man, a very rich man indeed.

For about four months after his brother left, Bobby's simple life consisted of waking up, going into the living room and watching television, and then watching television in bed until falling asleep. There was also breakfast, lunch, and dinner, which he ate in the living room in front of the television. This schedule was punctuated by visits to the bathroom and occasional trips to his lawyer's office until they received the settlement check. There were also interviews and other mandatory things involving the outside world, but these things became rarer and rarer, and he mostly just escaped into the world of movies, television shows, and just sitting and thinking, almost always about Daisy. He missed her so much, and every so often, either in his dreams or while he was sitting in the dark with the television on, he would remember that image that he could never forget. The image of Daisy's face when the thing, the pirate, squeezed that oversized, bony hand around her tiny little head. Her eyes bulging out, like she was in some Saturday morning cartoon or something. He continued to be haunted by the memories and could not bring himself to join the outside world yet. Then, in the sixth month after he left the hospital, he heard the sloshing sounds for the first time.

He was in the shower, water just turned off, and reaching for the towel when he heard it. It was a wet sloshing across the hardwood just beyond the bathroom door. He stood still inside the shower, hand extended for the towel, just listening. Then the sound moved into the living room, and then it just stopped. It took him thirty minutes before he was able to open the door and search the house. He hadn't found anything that time. Two days later, he heard it again. Lying on his side in bed, facing away from the open door leading into the hallway, he heard the sloshing footsteps moving across the hardwood floor in the living room and then coming closer, down the hallway.

Then the sloshing stopped. He heard the creak of the wood and heard Checkers meow in the hall.

Was it the cat this whole time? In that moment, he rolled over, expecting to see that stupid cat, and his whole body shook with horror at what he saw. In the dim light, he could make out the black shorts and white t-shirt. Water dripped from her arms, and though her face hid in shadows, he could see her smiling, and he knew it was Daisy.

The smell hit him all at once, and he gagged in the bed, almost puking. It stood there, still as a dark statue for a few seconds, and then it turned and sloshed back the way it had come, across the hardwood floors, away from him and down the hallway. He heard the front door open and close, and then remained in bed, still frozen in fear for several minutes, just staring out into the empty hallway.

The house was silent once again. Then Checkers meowed in the living room and he could hear the cat scratching on the closed front door, meowing for his mommy. He had locked the front door like he always did, so it wouldn't do any good to get up and lock it again. Either he was going crazy, or the thing was real; and if it *was* real, then it could get inside whenever it wanted.

When the sun came up, he moved into the living room and turned on the television. He stared at the front door out of the corner of his eye all day long, half expecting it to fling open at any minute. But it did not. When night fell, he stayed in the living room, where he felt slightly safer. He wasn't going into that bed again. Bobby considered getting into bed and closing the door, but he could imagine her swinging it open, and then he'd have to look into that hallway, and he just didn't think that was something he was willing to ever do again.

It had been dark less than an hour when he heard the voice in his head.

Bobby.

It sounded like Daisy, but was slightly deeper than he remembered. He tried to ignore it, turning the volume up on the television.

Bobby.

This time, the voice was softer, more like the wife he had known. He could sense something in the backyard, drawing him, pulling him there. He turned off the television and walked into the kitchen. As he approached the small, square windows on the back door, he could see her figure sitting at the table on the back porch. They had sat at that table so many times and drank, having long talks for hours. Their friends had come over and sat at that very table and talked to them under that very umbrella. The face of the thing hid in shadows, and he stepped up to the back door, face to the glass, and took a closer look.

Bobby.

As he tried to decide whether to go to his wife or not, Checkers meowed beneath him. He picked the cat up to lock him up in the bedroom.

Can I see my baby? Please, Bobby. Bring him with you.

He held the cat tighter as his other hand turned the knob and he stepped outside into the dark.

No light.

He closed the door and sat down in the darkness, but he could see her. She was still smiling, and she had black holes where eyes should be. Even in the shadows, he could see enough.

"I'm here," he whispered. "Is it really you?"

Yes.

He thought for a few minutes about what to ask her, petting Checkers and trying not to look across the table. Finally, he spoke.

"What do you want?"

I love you.

He needed to know what it wanted. He had to know if he was crazy.

"No, I know you love me. I love you too." He was crying now. "I need to know what you want from me. Why are you here?"

I want to be with you. I know it cannot be like before. I can stay outside if you want.

His eyes were drawn to the little shed in the backyard.

I'll stay there. If you ever want me, just come outside. I won't come into the house again. Not unless you want me to.

"I don't." Bobby could barely breathe, and his stomach turned.

I understand. I love you, Bobby. I'm your wife, and I love you very much. I just want us to be a family again. That's all.

"I don't think that can happen." The smell hit him hard. He winced, and the tears fell. "I'm going back inside now. I love you too. I love you too, Daisy."

He stood up quickly and rushed through the door, slamming and locking it behind him. He let Checkers jump to the floor and he stared out the window. It had stood up and was walking across the back yard. He watched as it stopped and just sat down in the grass, facing the house, his wife staring back at him through that glass. He turned away from her, and he remembered her face; not the one on the porch just now, and not the one with the cartoon eyes. He remembered the face on the streets of Manila, that face that had kissed him on that empty sidewalk, and he smiled for the first time in as long as he could remember. Bobby even let out a little laugh, and he didn't feel as afraid anymore as he unlocked the door and went to bed.

He was lying on his side in the bed, wide awake, when he heard the back door open, the footsteps sloshing through the house, the creak of the hardwood in the hallway, and then he shuddered as he felt something get into the bed. He could feel the wetness against his bare back, and the slimy little arms wrapped around his waist, and then it whispered, both in his head and in his ear.

I love you.

He closed his eyes and remembered her face.

"I love you too."

***

Somewhere deep in the depths of the ocean, the two scientists were walking along the rocky floor. They stopped and faced one another.

Did you see it?

Yes. I saw it.

Praise Thing.

Praise Thing.

The two things turned their bodies and walked, then floated, back to their laboratory in the cave.

The Detective

by Jason Fischer

Pete did not like the man who owned the shoe repair shop. It wasn't for a tangible reason, it was for something that was much harder to dismiss. It was a hunch. Pete was a retired detective. It was a forced retirement due to alcohol abuse after losing his wife, not the honorable kind.

As he leaned against the brick wall of the mall's east corridor, trying to look inconspicuous, he stared at the face of a man who looked desperate. No matter how hard he tried, Pete could not shut down the sensors that laid dormant in his mind for so very long. He had learned through long and hard training that the sense that brought him financial success and kept him upright was not to be ignored when it was this loud.

The shoe repair owner had an uncaring grin on his face as he talked to his customer. From this distance, Pete would put the shop owner's height at five foot even. His head appeared to be twice the size it should be. It was so large Pete wondered if it was hard for his rail-thin body to support it. He could barely hear anything, but from his body language the customer appeared to be screaming.

Remnants of the yell echoed through the nearly empty corridor. It was just Pete and a few of his fellow mall walkers an hour before the shopping mall officially opened.

Pete could see the satisfaction on the little man's face. Whatever was happening between them, he was enjoying the other man's apparent suffering. Nothing was adding up, which in Pete's experience meant trouble. Out of habit, his hand went to his side, looking for the reassurance of a holster that hadn't been there in well over a year. He chuckled slightly to himself, feeling more useless than usual, making him wish he had been on time today. Normally by now he would have been off to his house for a quick shower, but he hit the snooze button a few too many times after a late night. Sleep was becoming a contest again. One he was not winning. It wasn't surprising. He was coming up on the anniversary of his wife's death. Not having adequate coping skills and intentionally staying away from liquor, the vicious game with sleep was his subconscious' way of saying he was hurting and couldn't run any longer.

The nagging feeling like he was regressing had been weighing him down for longer than he would like to admit. After nearly a year of self-loathing, Pete got himself back together. Making peace with his life without Kate was not something he was quite capable of—they were married a year outside of high school and would have stayed that way if not for the heart attack—but he learned to at least compartmentalize it in the same way he did with his work.

Routine got him this far. A steady regiment of walking every day was part of his new wellness habit. At his age, if anyone from his old life knew how Pete got his exercise in the winter months, which in Illinois felt like half the year, he would die from embarrassment. To go from running security and investigations for the largest legal firm in Chicago to being a mall walker and spending five afternoons volunteering at the donation center, sorting through the various junk and hauling it to other regions, would be beyond comprehension for anyone from his former life.

For Pete, it was simple work, and it filled precious time. It did just enough to keep the nagging thoughts at bay. The desire to get back into the game never fully extinguished, but he kept it at an almost-manageable level. At least it was, until the final few laps, when he first saw the man who was slowly becoming an obsession. If the store's rolling gate had just been down on his last lap, he would have never had stopped at the store he had passed a million times.

Calling on his training, Pete took in not only the man, but every detail of his small storefront. The store was rundown with a long U-shaped counter spanning the length of the three walls. The owner's head was his most distinguishing feature. It was nearly perfectly round and twice the size it should be, big enough that it caused him to lean significantly forward. He had eyebrows so thick they could be mistaken for mustaches. The hair on his head was a very dark brown, almost black, with no graying. Yet, by the deep-set wrinkles marking his face, Pete would put him well into his eighties. If forced to give a one-word description, Pete would say the man looked like a troll from a fairy tale. Like the characters from those fables, the little man could be good or evil. Pete believed it was the latter. This was not a rational thought, but he would bet with any odds that he was right.

As he watched the customer leave the store with his right hand wrapped in what looked like a stained wet cloth, Pete reminded himself that there was no upside to taking his obsession further. It took more willpower than it should have, but he continued his walk. While exiting the mall, he cussed internally for running so late. He hustled to get back home to shower, shave, and get to work.

***

Four days later, his curiosity had become an uncontrollable obsession. He knew it resulted from boredom and he should let it go, but this was an itch he was determined to scratch. Maddeningly, there was no real interest in what was going on in the shop. Pete didn't care if the man was running a prostitution ring, he just needed to know if his instincts could still be trusted.

Trying to be practical, he chose a pair of his wife's high heels in need of repair. He wasn't anywhere near ready to give away her old clothes, but knew one day he would donate them, so it wasn't a completely frivolous act. Somehow, that gave him the slight reassurance that all he carefully held together wasn't becoming completely unraveled.

That afternoon, with the heels under his arm, Pete entered the store.

"Good afternoon, sir. What can I help you with today?" The little man had a refined voice with a melodious cadence. He looked up at Pete with a practiced smile beaming from his misshapen head.

"I was hoping you could repair these." Removing them from the canvas bag, he placed the red heels on the counter.

The shopkeeper lifted the shoes, closely inspecting the loose heel with his odd fingers. Like his head, the very tips were twice the size of the fingers, giving them the appearance of lollipops. With amazing dexterity in spite of the deformity, the man slightly peeled back the leather edge of the shoe. Satisfied with what he saw, he replied, "Yes, I believe we can do that. When do you need them back?"

Pete adjusted his gaze from the man's fingers to meet his eyes. They were dull and lacked focus, reminding Pete of staring at a dog. "How long do you think it'll take?"

"It shouldn't take more than an hour. I could easily have them ready for you to pick up tomorrow."

"I'd be willing to wait if you can work on them now." The cobbler looked perturbed in the way a man who was asked to forfeit something valuable would. Ignoring this, Pete added, "It would save me a trip back."

In his gentle tone, the shopkeeper said, "Are you sure it wouldn't be more convenient to get them tomorrow?"

Having no concern if he was putting the man out, Pete quickly said, "No, now is perfect, if you have the time."

Glancing at the wall clock, the tiny man said with a sigh, "Well, if you insist, I can accommodate." With an unexpected swiftness, the little man disappeared into the darkness of the back room. It was presumably his workshop; however, nothing was visible through the arched opening.

The next forty minutes were spent in measured boredom. Pete could neither see into the work room nor hear anything useful other than the intermittent sound of hammering. The store itself had very little to draw Pete's attention. The butcher block counter was bare except for an oversized calculator and an empty notepad. Beneath a portion of the counter that ran parallel with the three walls were overpriced shoelaces and cleaners sitting on dirty shelves. A painting of a cottage in a meadow and a clock were the only items adorning the walls. By the quality of the work, it was an easy assumption that the owner painted it, or someone close to him had.

Having nowhere to sit, he leaned against the counter, staring out into the mall corridor. Eight shoppers passed the store, none even glancing in his direction. The mall's security guard—Pete recognized him from his morning walks—passed the store in half-hour intervals. Wearing a cheap uniform that didn't look like it had ever been pressed, the geriatric patrolman gave a slight wave each time he made his rounds.

Not a single soul entered the store. It wasn't like he was expecting to have a drug mule make a drop right in front of him, but he would welcome anything at this point.

As the minutes ticked by, Pete realized that he had far too much time on his hands. Indulging his boredom by wasting his afternoon made him feel very foolish and older than his forty-four years.

Finally, the shopkeeper reemerged with the shoes wrapped in a plastic bag. All the color was missing from his face. Straining, he placed the package on the counter. "That will be fourteen dollars, please."

Politely, Pete replied, "Are you sure that's all?"

"Yes, sir. It was a...simple repair. The shoes are of very good quality."

For what they cost, they should be. His wife was a very frugal woman, despite their income. One of her only indulgences was her shoes. He handed the man his money. "It's an interesting job you have. How'd you learn your trade?"

The man took the money and put it presumably in a lockbox. The counter concealed his hands, making it impossible to tell. Completing his task, he grabbed the notepad. "It's a family business going back several generations. May I have your name and address for the receipt?"

Pete gave the address of his former employer to keep the conversation going. He smiled, thinking of the law firm that handled the clientele of politicians and people of influence getting flyers from the cobbler. "These days it must be rough. Most things are made so cheap I would think people just toss them instead of having them repaired."

This sparked interest in the man. He raised his head and spoke in a slightly deeper tone. "I suppose this is true, but don't dismiss sentimental value. I would assume you can remember all the good times you had with your wife when she used to be able to wear these. That is what keeps us open. There are many who want to relive these experiences."

Pete's eye twitched, and he felt sweat trickle down his sides. The man's stare somehow drew Pete in. "What do you mean when she *used* to be able to wear these?" Pete's eyes became tiny slits as he stared at him.

"How could she walk or dance with the loose heel?"

His facial expression betrayed the odd man's verbal response. Pete had the impression he somehow knew his wife was not alive. It was a preposterous thought, but it hung there firing once-familiar synapses in his mind that were long dormant. "Oh, of course." Before he could get another question in, a young woman entered the store wearing skintight clothing, complementing her exaggerated figure. She looked as if she could use forty hours of sleep. It would vastly improve her color and the bags under her eyes.

Tilting his head to his next customer, the little man tore the sales slip and handed Pete the carbon copy. "Is there anything else I can do for you today?"

Knowing he had lost the opportunity to disguise his conversation as small talk, Pete said, "No. Thank you for taking care of this." When he walked away, he got a better look at the woman. Despite looking haggard, she was very pretty. Leaving her here with the odd man felt wrong somehow. As she approached the counter, he noticed a slight limp, and two fingers on her left hand were missing. Pete left the store having no more a true sense of the man he knew was bad than he had an hour ago.

***

That evening, Pete got in touch with the last connection he had to his former career, Jupiter Johnson. The man named after the planet—his father was a hippie with an astronomy fetish—was glad to take his call. Pete asked him to run a quick check on the shopkeeper, no questions asked. An hour later, he called Pete back with his research.

"Yeah, so I don't feel like I'm doing you much of a favor here, buddy."

"I'll let you know that." Pete let out a quick laugh. "What'd you get, Jupe?"

"The owner's name is Wolfgang Addais, eighty-four years old. Besides his colorful name, he is the least interesting man in the world. He's run his business in the mall from the day it opened in 1978. Previously, the business was located forty miles from its current location under the same name of Cobbler's Corner. His finances are unremarkable. He pays his taxes and vendors on time, no children or any previous significant history. There isn't even a single complaint to the Better Business Bureau against his company."

After giving him the rundown, Jupiter was awkwardly silent.

"Yeah, you're right. That wasn't much of a favor."

"Screw off, jackass."

Jupiter laughed hard enough to sting Pete's ear. "Seriously, man, I appreciate it."

"No reason to say thanks, but if you insist, how about we meet up at Cozy Corner and eat a cheap steak and have a few beers?"

Pete knew his old partner was intently fishing to force him out of the house. Seeing Pete for dinner had become a familiar tug of war.

They hadn't gotten together for months. Pete felt a tinge of guilt as he said, "Going to have to raincheck, bud." He was scanning from his standard excuse list in his mind, intent to not use the same one as last time, when his friend saved him the trouble.

"It's okay, I understand. Getting late anyway. Take care of yourself, alright?"

"Yes, sir."

That evening he kept himself distracted with the help of frozen pizza and the television. He once again stayed up beyond his normal bedtime, wrestling with his obsession with the shopkeeper.

***

In the middle of the night, there was a rustling, pulling Pete from his sleep. It came from somewhere in the center of the bedroom. Barely awake, Pete rolled over and saw the plastic bag moving across the carpeted floor. The thin, almost translucent plastic was being dragged behind the high-heeled shoes. The heels slid across the floor in a jerky stop-motion way, inching toward the bathroom. Pete, still foggy from sleep, could only imagine that a mouse had gotten into the bag.

Not willing to watch anymore of the macabre march, he balled up the bedsheet and threw it. The makeshift net successfully covered his nighttime visitor. Carefully, he slid off the bed. Images of rodents scurrying to nip at his toes caused him to shiver. He quickly grabbed the umbrella propped against the dresser. Approaching the blanket, he could clearly see both shoes still moving beneath the thin fabric.

He swung at the shoes with the larger handle side, sending them toppling into the bathroom. He flicked on the bathroom light, fully expecting to see a furry creature come running out. Instead, he watched the heels wobble and then, with a rocking motion, once again become upright. They slowly walked to the closet inside the bathroom.

Pete slammed the closet door shut, feeling slightly dizzy. Seconds later, he could hear tapping and then a hanger rattling on the floor. He thought he heard a woman's voice faintly whisper, "Help me." Without hesitation, he whipped open the door, cocking his hand back into a fist.

On the floor lay a distorted version of his wife, wearing the shoes and a matching red dress. Somehow, she was a two-dimensional character resembling a life-sized cardboard cut-out. Her outline was pencil-thin and perfectly flat. The living photo's eyes and mouth moved as she cried out, "Help me, Pete."

There was no doubt it was her voice. It was exactly the same tone and pitch that had been echoing in his head since she passed. Instinct won out of fear, driving him to bend down to grab her.

The moment he made contact, her body inflated. In waves from head to shoes, what once looked like an oversized photo slowly took shape like a balloon as air was forced into it. As the transformation made its way to her face, he pulled her to his bare chest, and she threw her arms around him. After the embrace, she wept. When he felt her warm tears, Pete knew this wasn't a dream or a momentary delusion. His Kate was back from the dead.

Wordlessly, they stared into each other's eyes. Pete felt like he could see into her thoughts. The effort seemed to prevent him from speaking. Slowly, he stood, pulling her up. She was as light as a sheet of paper.

All he knew at this point was that the shoes had somehow brought her back. He couldn't understand it, yet there could be no other explanation. As he pulled her back toward the bed, he knew Kate had no awareness of ever being gone. It was a sense stronger than any intuition he had ever experienced. With every passing second, the overwhelming fear that she would disappear lessened. This at least made it slightly easier to wait to find the right words to ask his dead spouse.

As he became slightly more comfortable, he caressed her hand and forearm. She did not feel the same. There was resistance when his fingers made contact, and when he applied even slight pressure, her form would reshape. It was like placing a finger in a bowl of syrup. His touch would cause a rippling effect that retracted to its original shape when removed. As he continued to examine her, she slightly pulled back and looked bashfully at him.

Feeling her embarrassment, he quickly stopped. Beyond the physical changes to her skin, she was exactly as he remembered. He felt something solid in his throat as he fought out the words he had held in. "How...are you here?"

Sitting on the bed, she tucked her legs beneath her, pulling the dress taught across her hips. He could smell the slight aroma of coconut from her skin and conditioner in her hair. It was staggering to him how he had forgotten how she smelled. Finding himself lost in her, he hated himself for all the times he took her for granted. She smiled the smile that always made him feel like the most important person in the world before saying, "Where else would I be?"

Swallowing hard, tears stung his eyes. "You don't know what it's been like." The final word cracked, making his chest hitch. His insides ached, as if all the pain he had bottled up suddenly became uncorked. Fighting the wave of emotions, his gut quivered, and his fingers trembled.

"Oh, please don't cry, Pete."

He leaned in to hug her. She pulled back with a look of terror, saying, "Please, I don't know what you are talking about."

Her nose seemed to flatten as if it was being eaten by her face. Pete sat up straight, trying to wish away the transformation. "Please, no! We don't have to talk about that...right now."

The second he touched her hand, her smile came back, and her face slowly went back to its original shape.

"Have you eaten?"

She looked over her shoulder, glancing at the clock. With a laugh, she asked, "Why are we up?"

Ignoring how odd she felt, he grabbed her other hand and pulled them near his chest. "I'm up so I can stare at your beauty."

"Ah, so charming, darling." She leaned in and kissed his cheek.

Her lips felt like cold gelatin. Fighting the urge to kiss her on the lips, he wrestled with his frantic mind, trying to find the right question. Finally, he let go and asked, "Did you say you were hungry?"

"Starving! How about my strawberry pancakes?"

Pete could taste the butter on them, making him salivate as his mind replayed their many Sunday mornings eating in the kitchen nook.

"Race you to the kitchen!" She pulled away from him and got off the bed.

Instantly, he felt as if a piece of him was missing. Watching her walk, she began slowly shrinking back to her two-dimensional form. The dress looked like it was floating on a hanger. Panicked, Pete got off the bed and grabbed her hand. By the time they were in the kitchen, she was fully formed once again.

***

Over the next few days, Pete learned to accept the unbelievable. During that time, offering no explanation, she refused to let Pete leave the house. When he pressed, she would cry uncontrollably, sobbing, "This will end," repeatedly. The outbursts were the only recognition that she had any knowledge of the arrangement. As difficult as it was, he pressed her at these times for answers. He wasn't proud of himself, but he saw no other choice. Watching the depth of her pain as she cried, and the horrified look in her eyes, he quickly found he was not up to putting her through any further interrogations.

Every morning, thinking the entire experience might have been a dream, he would blindly reach across the bed, expecting her to be gone. Part of him wished it was when he saw the terrifying, paper-thin image of Kate drifting back and forth. Her lips were the only part of her that had any depth. They protruded out as she would whisper, "Sorry." After a frightful few minutes of holding her hand—it draped over his like a rope—she would regain her form once again.

The memory of her two-dimensional form scared him deeply, to the point he wouldn't trust his reaction if he ever saw her that way again. She never left his side. Free moments were now measured in seconds, not minutes, and when he found them, he repeatedly called the shoe repair shop. Each call yielded the same result. The phone was never answered and there was no voicemail. After several days, he stopped trying.

Their extraordinary situation was slowly filled with very ordinary activities. Most of their time was spent talking over extravagant meals and watching old movies on television. To his own astonishment, hours would go by where Pete would forget the reality of the situation. In the darkness the height of winter brought, day and night no longer meant anything to them. Without a single distraction beyond the walls of their home, they grew closer, never thinking of any entanglements of the outside world.

The newfound contentment ended precisely two weeks after it began. That morning, he woke up and reached for Kate. His fingertips only found her empty dress. After two days, he realized she wasn't coming back.

***

The next morning, after realizing she was gone possibly for good, at twenty minutes before the mall's opening, Pete sat in his car watching the entrance. For the fourth time, he checked the ammo in his gun. The automatic was the same one he used to carry when he was paid to help the influential out of whatever trouble they put themselves in. From this position, he could see the front of the store through the mall's corridor. The pull-down gate was still closed.

Next to him in the passenger seat was his suitcase. It had a travel lock on it and was wrapped in a belt, the shoes and red dress its only contents. He was afraid to take it out of the house, thinking that it might alter her as she warned him previously, that they could not leave, but there was little choice. It took a lot to fight the logical part of himself, questioning how the little troll of a man brought her back and, even worse, what if it wasn't him? Pete was not a religious man. He did not believe in anything beyond what he could see and feel, but he couldn't stop wondering if this was a spiritual experience. He was given Kate again and now she was taken away, possibly as some sort of penance.

At ten on the dot, he entered the store with the suitcase in hand and was greeted by Wolfgang. "Mr. Crenshaw, I was expecting you."

The words stopped Pete in his tracks. He had thought of his approach for the last hour. There wasn't a single scenario in which he thought it would start like this. In a very quiet voice, he mumbled, "Why?"

"We both know why you are here." His eyes went to the suitcase. Pete started to interrupt, and the little man held up his misshapen hand. In a rehearsed way, he went on as if he was discussing a dinner menu instead of an undead woman. "I can save us both a lot of time if you please allow me to explain. I cannot give you answers to the questions that you seek."

"So...you know." Saying it out loud to this man felt somehow humiliating. "Know she came back?"

"Yes."

"So, when I left here the last time, you knew this was going to happen?" The man nodded. Feeling equal relief and resentment, Pete loudly said, "How's this possible?"

"You can ask a thousand times and the answer will always be the same. You have been given a gift and I am only the messenger."

"What do you know?" Pete placed both hands on the counter, leaning forward, trying to appear as if he had some control, or at least as if he could take it.

"That sometimes my tools can bring back the lost." The small man slowly turned over his right hand and shrugged his shoulder.

"So, it doesn't happen for everyone?"

"No, I don't get to choose."

Pete did not want to ask the next question. "Was this a onetime thing?"

"No."

"So, you can bring her back?"

"Of course."

The relief instantly released the tension in his shoulders until he looked back at the man. Pete did not like the look on the man's face.

Placing the suitcase carefully on the counter, he asked, fighting himself to not beg, "Can you do it right now?"

"That depends on what you are willing to bargain with."

At that moment, he knew the hunch that brought him here was right.

Pete flipped the hinged counter over and shoved the little troll into the back room. It was bare except for a massive table holding peculiar instruments, the largest being a wooden sewing machine. He slammed the little man against the table, pinning him there, and pulled his gun from the back of his pants. He pushed it under his chin. The shop owner smelled of decay as he hissed, "Do it." He snapped at Pete's nose, missing by only a fraction of an inch. The action was animalistic. Breathing deeply through his nose, Wolfgang flippantly said, "Understand, anything you do to me, I will do to her."

"Not if you're dead."

"Then you will never see her again. Do as you will." With the blunt declaration, the troll slapped away Pete's arm and carefully straightened out his tailored suit with his misshapen fingers. "I appreciate the position you are in, Mr. Crenshaw. You have a very difficult choice to make. For this reason, I will forgive your outburst, but just this one time."

He wanted to pull the trigger so badly it was as if his hand had a will of its own. The satisfaction of taking away the confident smile was almost worth not seeing Kate again. He kicked the desk full force, scattering the cobbler's instruments, letting out an insane guttural moan.

"There is always so much anger in your kind. You should learn to appreciate the gift that you have been offered."

Fidgeting, he looked back through the door into the mall. The corridor was completely empty. Pete tightly squeezed the handle of the gun. The weight felt familiar, bringing comfort. Looking back at the little man, he said, "What do you want?"

"For my services, you will give me all of your toenails." He bared his crooked teeth as he smiled.

For the first time, the realization came that he was not dealing with a human being. Pete raised the gun once more, squeezing the butt. In disbelief, he nearly yelled, "What did you say?"

"I am not in the habit of repeating myself, so listen carefully. You will bring me your full toenails wrapped in a cloth in a pair of your dress shoes. Once I receive them, I will once again bring your wife back to you." Very carefully he straightened his tie. Once it was in place, he brought his eyes slowly upward, staring directly at Pete. "I will warn you that if you don't do this within four hours, she will cease to exist in either this or the spiritual realm."

After everything he had experienced, he knew the troll was telling the truth. The realization brought a helplessness he had not experienced since he was told of his wife's passing. Adrenaline shot through him, making his fingers tingle. Knowing he needed more time to think, he took a deep, cleansing breath. With his head spinning, he decided he had to keep him talking as he processed all that was happening. "If I pay your price, will she be here permanently?"

"I will give you one month before the next installment." Looking at Pete's reaction, he said, "Save the anger and indignation, Mr. Crenshaw, it will not help you."

Despair took over in a wave as Pete once again lowered the gun. Fighting the instinct to ask what happened after a month, Pete walked slowly out of the dark work room, leaving the shoes on the counter.

Wolfgang called out. "Don't forget, Mr. Crenshaw, time is of the essence."

Not having the energy to look at the man for another second, he left the store, walking slowly.

***

Sitting on the concrete stoop of his garage, after much consideration, he peeled off the first toenail with a pair of industrial specialty pliers in a constant sideways motion instead of one hard yank. Even with the Novocaine he injected, there was a shock wave of pain that traveled up his leg into his stomach. The second the nail released from the cuticle with a revolting tearing noise, he didn't know if he could continue. Knowing anticipation would heighten the fear, he moved to the second toe. He'd decided to go larger to small, leaving the big toe for last, thinking it would bring the most resistance and possibly cause him to black out.

This time, he altered his approach and yanked with all his strength. Quickly, he realized this was a tragically bad idea. The nail snapped in an uneven piece across his exposed flesh, leaving less than half still attached. Wheezing, he bent and dug the pliers into the oozing, newly exposed flesh. This eclipsed the worst pain he had ever experienced. Carefully, in several attempts—the nose of the pliers kept slipping free, digging into delicate soft tissue—he removed the partial nail.

Shaking, he sat looking at his exposed toes, not knowing if he had the strength to continue. Feeling weaker than he ever had in his life, he sat on his garage floor, trying to recoup his strength. One thought kept him going. Once she was safely back, he would figure out how to get revenge on the monster. The anger kept him sharp as he completed his painful chore, one tearing inch at a time.

Shuffling into the store with his feet wrapped in gauze, Pete wordlessly handed his payment to the troll. He could feel his heartbeat in the tips of his toes as he stood staring at the smirking figure behind the counter. The pain was excruciating, but he was determined to not show it. Wolfgang wordlessly took his prize into the back room, once again disappearing into the darkness.

The last few hours had felt unreal, like watching someone else's dream. Somehow, they felt even more unreal than Kate coming back. In his delirium, he couldn't decide if he would have been better off never meeting this man. Of course, that meant he would have never seen Kate again, and in his weakened state he thought that might have been for the best.

After a short while, he heard the muffled sound of tools being used in the back room. In less than twenty minutes, the little man emerged with the red high heels. He placed them on the counter.

"As you have kept your word, I shall keep mine, Mr. Crenshaw. You have precisely one month before we will meet again. I must warn you that if you have the illusion that you can persuade me to give you more time, you will learn a very hard lesson. The severity of your next payment will be determined by your behavior. If I see you before the month is up, there will be consequences."

Pete noticed one of his toenails dangling at the side of the troll's mouth like a toothpick. It made his stomach turn. He grabbed the shoes and did his best to walk out of the store without causing more damage to his toes. When he was almost out of earshot, he heard, "It's been a pleasure doing business with you."

***

The next morning, Kate was back. He fought back tears at the relief. Once again, she began as a two-dimensional figure. As unnatural as it felt, he hugged her tightly, feeling her shape contour to his body.

She was slowly getting her shape back as she smiled. "Well, isn't that the best way to start the day?" She playfully kissed his nose.

As she walked out of the bedroom, he watched her hair bounce with each step. From this vantage point, she looked as if she was her old self. Not wanting her to deflate, Pete pulled the sheet back and placed his feet on the floor. Immediate sharp pain ran up his legs, reminding him of his chore. He glanced at his white socks, the tips stained red with his blood. Carefully, he made his way out of the bedroom to join his now two- dimensional wife in the window nook.

Over the next few days, Kate spent a good deal of time staring at her husband's limp. She never mentioned it and would look hastily away if he caught her noticing. It was truly what he would have asked for, not wanting to explain, but somehow he could not help but feel hurt by her silence. No matter how hard he tried, Pete could not distance himself from these comparisons, old Kate versus new Kate. Everything felt off. Slowly, he knew the derision of his mind was being driven by his resentment at having to degrade himself to the troll of a man. Equally unable to allow himself to be beholden to the man and knowing there would be no life without Kate, Pete considered his options.

After two weeks, Pete knew it was time to get to work. The next payment was coming due. Knowing that he couldn't threaten the man without adequate leverage, he started the surveillance. He chose Bruce Andrews, a P.I. that he used to contract for basic jobs. After a few days, he quickly learned that the reports were not worth the daily fee. There were no repeat customers to follow, and the little man spent nearly all his time standing behind the counter, never using the phone. After a few days, Bruce followed him to his home at night; no visitors or notable activity. With no other leads, the only option was to search the shopkeeper's home. Bruce was competent for surveillance work, but for the search, Pete knew he would have to do it himself.

The first obstacle was leaving Kate alone. He had brought up his need to leave to her a few times, and the conversation went as expected. The tantrums were intolerable. Having no way to loosen her up with alcohol—he had found that since she came back, drinking did nothing to her—he knew he had no choice but to go with a direct approach. With five days before the next installment, Pete had his backpack prepared with the necessary equipment to perform his search. He grabbed her by the arm and told her he had no choice but had to run out for work. With tears pouring out of her eyes, she tried to hold him in place. It made his heart feel like it was going to burst, but he pulled away from her, causing her hands to come apart. She groped at him with her fingers elongated from his retraction. Quickly, without looking back, as he did not trust himself to go if he allowed her pain to penetrate, he left through the front door. As it slammed, he could still hear her cries.

Pete felt empty as he drove toward Wolfgang's house. There were light flurries to add to the two feet of aging snow. Less than two miles from his destination, he texted Bruce. The P.I. was in the mall watching the shop and would alert Pete if the troll left for any reason. It probably wasn't necessary. The shop didn't close for another hour, but there was no reason to take a chance. The text came back that all was clear.

A little less than a half-mile away, Pete parked on the dark street. Grabbing his backpack, he walked the rest of the way, staying on the freshly plowed street. He hadn't been out walking in weeks and, despite his mood, the exercise felt good, even if his toes were aching. Most of the surrounding homes were abandoned long ago when the interstate came through. The arched highway ran over the tiny neighborhood perched on massive concrete supports. Wolfgang's house was directly below the apex of the bridge. It was the cottage in the painting that hung in the shoe repair shop. It was as unimpressive as its artistic representation.

Pete made his way to the backdoor. There was no security system. The lock was as basic as they came. He made short work of it with his pick. Once inside, he was glad to see a light on in the living room, eliminating his need for a flashlight. As was his usual procedure, he made a cursory search to be sure he was alone. The house was a tiny ranch home with only five rooms. All were clear, except for the bedroom. Lying in the corner was the mangiest dog he had ever seen. It looked more like an overgrown rat than a canine. When Pete entered the room, it barely raised its head. It just stared with its human-like eyes and went back to sleep.

He began the search. In the bottom drawer of the dresser were several handwritten letters. Unfortunately, they were in what he believed to be German. He took photos of all of them with his phone and placed the letters back, careful to put them in the same position as he'd found them, then left the sad room. The main room didn't have a TV; only a couch, a rocking chair, and a table. It was made from the same wood as the one in the shop. He entered the small bathroom. There was a dirty shower stall and no toilet. The hole where it used to be was exposed and caked in dust and a sticky substance. The odd little man apparently took care of his business outdoors. In the kitchen, the only utensils and plates were made of wood and covered in a thick varnish. Inside the fridge was a single bottle of vodka with a label that was unique to Pete, written in illegible calligraphy.

Feeling less and less confident that he was going to uncover anything useful, Pete crawled through the tiny door that led to the attic. Once inside, he turned on his mini flashlight, illuminating a dirty, claustrophobic stairway that smelled of age and dust. It was so narrow that he had to turn sideways as he walked. Clearing the stairs, he was in the attic. The ceiling wasn't high enough for him to stand. Carefully, he straddled the ceiling joists. Balancing on their narrow surface brought a sharp pain to his toes.

Four steps across, his phone buzzed, startling him and almost causing him to lose his balance. Regaining his foothold, Pete looked at his watch, hoping he hadn't lost track of time. Glancing at the screen, it was his friend Kel, making his weekly call. It was a relief that it wasn't a warning that Wolfgang was on his way. Pete hit the ignore button, letting it go to voicemail.

Back to the search, he came across two sheets of plywood at the end of the room laid over the joists. At the center was a handmade wooden box. The craftmanship was impeccable. Inside the box were polaroid photos. The photos were a mixture of very old-looking shoes and assorted mannequin parts. Pete slowly inspected each one; imagining the footwear bringing back the dead made his stomach turn. Glad to be through with them, he returned them to the box. As he had done in every other room, he exhaustively searched for a possible hidden panel, finding nothing. He left the house through the door he entered, locking it behind him as he left. The only hope now was that the letters had some type of useful information.

When Pete got back, Kate lay on the floor perfectly flat. As he kneeled beside her, he forced himself to look directly at her face; it was unsettling. Looking at her face reminded him of the photos he viewed in the attic of the plastic woman. "I'm so sorry, but you must believe me. I had to go."

Sitting up, she smiled the same as the first time he saw her, her lips and mouth projected beyond the flat face. "I'm just glad you're back."

He grabbed what should have been her hand, helping her up. As she stood, she wrapped her arms around him, clinging to him like a wet towel. Trying to not show his repulsion, he slowly disentangled from her, and they walked to the bedroom.

He undressed as Kate sat on the bed, watching his every movement. She had little strength, swaying in place as if a gentle breeze could move her easily. He was eager to translate the letters, but was exhausted. The spent adrenaline had finally run its way through him. Getting into his sleeping clothes, he was overwhelmed with guilt. Looking over his shoulder, he couldn't understand why she hadn't re-inflated yet. He knew his leaving had caused her to look the way she did, and could only hope in the morning she would get back to normal. When he sat on the bed, she draped her arm over his shoulder, and with her paper-like hand caressed the side of his face. He knew she wanted sex. The longing he came to know was in her eyes. Slowly, her hand drifted to his lap. Wordlessly, he pulled away and laid down. As he lay there, trying to avoid touching her thin body, he drifted off in less than a minute.

After a few hours of disturbed sleep, Pete awoke, knowing he was alone in bed. Through the dim moonlight, he saw Kate standing against the wall with her back to him. Almost whispering, he said, "Honey, what are you doing?" In a disturbing gesture, she soundlessly lifted her paper-thin arm in a sideways motion, pointing across the room. Suddenly there was a rotten smell assaulting him. He turned his head to see what his wife was pointing at.

Like a flash, the troll leaped and was on his chest, placing his misshapen hand over Pete's nose and mouth. Instinctively, he punched and wriggled, but the little man was like a stone, not budging an inch. He stared at his hypnotic glare, his face displaying neither happiness nor sadness. It had the neutrality of contentment. As Pete was desperately gasping for even a sliver of air, the man whispered, "It did not have to be like this, Mr. Crenshaw."

Minutes later, Pete was dead. The troll stepped down from the bed, carefully adjusting his suit. From his bag, he laid out a pressed suit for Pete and placed the dress shoes that Pete used to transport his toenails from his house to the store on top of it.

The funeral was small and held at the gravesite. There were no flowers or prayers as the casket was lowered into the ground. Attendance was small. Standing beside Jupiter were a few of Pete's friends from the donation center and a little man in an impeccably tailored suit. Jupiter did not like the look of the man and didn't bother with introductions, although he was curious how he knew his friend. The motor that lowered the casket whined as the wooden box made its final descent.

Inside the pitch-black space, Pete did not have the strength to scream. His cries were only a faint whisper dying into the fabric lining. Through a haze of panic, all he could hope for was that his new self was thin enough to slip between the crease of the casket. Pete had a debt to settle.

The Ocean at Night

BY STEPHEN RHOADES

IT WAS ALMOST NOON on a Sunday when I looked out the window of our cheap motel room to see my little red sedan with the motor running. A tiny pale hand gently touched my elbow as we drifted out the door and across the parking lot, not daring to turn toward the Driver. We got back on the road heading west, with my red sedan following closely behind.

Annie died in January of last year, and two months later I received the cardboard box from Tokyo. Annie was a sweet and kind woman. We met in college thanks to our shared interests in everything weird. We both loved oddities and spent most of our college money on taxidermy, bones, or other unique items associated with death. Then we got married, got jobs, had a baby, and by thirty we had a lot of weird shit we didn't want any of the other parents to see when they came over. So all of those items eventually found their way into my workshop, since it was in the basement and rarely seen.

I loved Annie so much, loved her more than I've ever loved another human being. With our daughter Charlotte grown up and in college, I knew it would be hard not to wallow in depression in that big house, all alone and surrounded by Annie's things. It took less than a month for me to realize that if I didn't figure out some way to go on living without her, I was going to die a miserable person; whether by alcohol or some other weapon, I knew I would find a way. I'm not saying that she saved my life. Lord knows that isn't the case. But, if it hadn't been for Emma, I may have never smiled again.

You need to understand a little something about me, about the man that is Frank Roberson. I've always enjoyed making things out of wood. My father taught me woodworking when I was a boy and I studied art in college. Annie was an Art major too. When I had to get a real job, I worked by day for the plant near the college, but at night when I got home, I went into the workshop and created little wooden people to sell in my friend's store.

Little wooden Indians, wooden children, dogs, cats; I would make all kinds of things. I could usually sell enough to the tourists that came through Mark's shop in downtown Asheville to pay for the materials. It was just a hobby, but it was also a passion. It was the greatest gift my father ever gave me. It was like I'd get all bottled up inside, and the only thing that would release the anxiety would be forming shapes out of wood.

When I was a teenager, I fell in love with my father's wood shop the first time I set eyes on it. Annie and I were just starting out when he passed away, but we had a garage and I was able to squeeze all of that dead man's equipment into it.

Eventually we got a bigger house, and my garage workshop soon became a basement one. I decorated it with most of our oddities, like the creepy hanging skeleton draped in a black hooded robe. There's a pillowcase underneath the hood that covers the skull, and a gas mask over the white cloth where the face should be. Annie had named that one "the Bishop." There was also the stuffed bear with the doll face, the open casket with the life-sized mummy inside, and Charlie, the four-foot-tall ventriloquist dummy with the roving eyes that always freaked everyone out.

On one side of the room was a table saw and wooden workbench, and on the other side were the life-sized creatures, jars with organs and dead creatures floating in formaldehyde, and the boxes... Stacks and stacks of boxes filled with items that Annie said we should sell one day if we ever got the time, which we never did.

It was into that big, empty house I retreated after Annie's funeral. Then, two months later, I carried the package from Tokyo into the basement, and opened it up in front of Charlie, the Bishop, the bear, and all the other freaks.

When I pulled out the deflated sex doll, it was not love at first sight. But after she was inflated, I noticed how soft her skin really was. The wig was made from human hair; long, flowing human hair. Her eyes were brown, and once I had her wearing the little skirt and top that Annie hadn't been able to fit into since our college days, I decided to give her a name.

With the lights off, it actually felt like a real person, inside and out. For the first week or two, I imagined it was Annie, and the fantasy worked. It took about three weeks before I decided on a name. It was the name of a girl from elementary school that I vaguely remembered being in love with. It only took another month before I fell completely in love with Emma.

I realized that having sex with a doll was quite unusual, and most people would never consider such a thing, but deep down I always knew that it would work because of my infatuation with them. I've made thousands of wooden dolls in my forty-six years of existence, and the idea of loving one never seemed that strange to me. It almost felt natural when I stopped pretending she was Annie and gave her a name of her own.

There I was, almost three months removed from the funeral, and madly in love with a blow-up doll that possessed softer skin than any human I had ever touched. Everything went alright for the next seven months, until the night just before Thanksgiving, when we were lying together in the dark, and I heard Emma whisper in my ear for the very first time.

Strange things had been happening prior to that, and I had been getting paranoid about the possibility before her voice confirmed it. Some nights—not all, but some—when I would come home from work, the doll would be lying naked on the floor of my workshop. It was strange, because I never left her out like that. I made the bed every morning and tucked her in tightly before I went to work. On that first night, I went into the bedroom expecting to see my lover, but she wasn't there. When I found her in the workshop, I had to scold her to never do that again. I didn't really think she could hear me, but I was just taking my frustration out on a doll and, for some reason, didn't ask myself how she had gotten there.

It took months before I finally used my brain and stepped out of my fantasy world for a moment. When I faced the facts, it was pretty simple to conclude that either someone was coming into my home and molesting her, or she was getting out of bed herself. Since I knew she wasn't alive, I had an alarm system installed to catch the intruder. The first night I came home to find Emma in the basement, there was no sign of a break-in, so I invested in security cameras. I set one up in every room of the house, including the workshop.

It only took two nights before I had to scold her again, and then we sat down together on the couch to watch the security footage, which is when I saw her move for the first time. The footage showed her floating off the bed, moving like a gust of wind was carrying her through the house and into the workshop. She drifted toward the workbench, out of view, but the noise of the table saw could clearly be heard on the video. I hadn't noticed any signs of usage in the past, but I decided to move the camera to face the workbench that night to see if I could get footage of Emma operating the saw.

For weeks the camera captured no movement, and I didn't find her in the workshop anymore. Then I stopped watching the videos altogether, even when I started finding her in the workshop again. I should have been afraid, but I just kept on pretending that the cameras didn't exist. I tried to forget about seeing her float through the house, and I refused to watch any more of that impossible footage.

Still, I couldn't help but stare at her in fear while she lay still, looking for signs of life in those huge, oversized eyes. But I saw none. Sure, if I had looked at the video footage, I probably would have seen her going all over the place while I was at work, but I couldn't do it. By that night in November, I had settled back into a comfort zone with Emma... And then she spoke.

She whispered something so soft and faint that I couldn't understand it. The same sounds over and over again. I didn't turn the light on, move a muscle, or otherwise disrupt her in any way. I just stayed awake and listened to the almost cooing sounds she made. By morning they became more intelligible, and I heard her whisper those first words... She said my name. Then there was a knock at the door. I had forgotten all about Charlotte coming over for Thanksgiving morning. I hid Emma in the closet and rushed to the unlocked front door, arriving just as it opened.

"Happy Thanksgiving, Daddy!" Charlotte yelled as she let herself in and bear-hugged me.

"Happy Thanksgiving, Mr. Roberson," Carl said. He had been Charlotte's boyfriend for over two years and still looked positively scared to death of me.

They hadn't sat down for ten seconds when the doorbell rang, and the holiday began. Soon the living room comprised Annie's sister, Donna, with her teenage daughter, Monica; my redneck brother, Marcus, chewing tobacco and spitting into a plastic bottle; his lovely wife, Sandy, and their two boys, twelve-year-old Derrick and fourteen-year-old Robbie. Then my parents appeared and the whole crew was there. Donna and Sandy had brought all the food, and they reheated everything while everyone else milled around the house.

I sat in the recliner when I noticed one of the boys going into my bedroom. I quickly ushered him out and closed the door.

"That's my private area, Robbie. You're not allowed in there."

"What are those things for?" Robbie pointed to a security camera.

"Oh, it's to spy on people. So I can see if someone tries to take something or go somewhere they're not supposed to."

Robbie looked deep in thought for a moment, and then leaned toward me and whispered, "Can I see the Bishop?"

We both snuck away from the others and went downstairs. We had to sneak away because Sandy and Marcus were born-again Christians, and they couldn't stand the things that Annie and I had collected over the years. Two years ago, Robbie had some nightmares about the puppet Charlie, and so he had been forbidden to come downstairs anymore during the holiday visits. But he would incessantly ask every holiday, and I had trouble saying no to my godson.

"Is that really a skeleton underneath the robes?" Robbie was standing directly in front of the thing called the Bishop, examining the gas mask. "How does someone breathe through something like that?"

"Yes, you can see the skeletal hands and feet dangling beneath." I pointed as he examined the thing. "You breathe slowly. You breathe through that thing very slowly, Robbie."

The boy giggled and walked over to Charlie, looking back at me for approval to pick him up. I nodded, and he lifted the puppet and turned it around.

"It's just a block of wood. It isn't real or anything," Robbie said, looking at me for assurance.

"Yes, it is just a block of wood. It's never been alive a day in its life." I went over to an open box next to Robbie and pulled out a heavy jar. "Now this...this was once a living thing."

I turned and bent down, holding the jar in front of us as the boy's eyes lit up.

"What is it?" he asked.

I turned it slowly as I spoke. "His name is Arnold. He's a baby pig, but this little guy isn't just your ordinary, everyday swine. Do you see those tiny arms and legs?"

The boy stared in amazement, counting the limbs until he was done. "It's got eight legs and three eyes."

"And two tails." I turned the jar around for him to see the pig's backside, but Robbie had quickly lost interest in it and moved across the basement, examining every strange item he came across.

"What's this?" Robbie yelled from across the room.

I put Arnold back in the box and turned to see Robbie tentatively reaching out to touch Emma's breast.

"Robbie, get away from her!" I rushed over and ushered the boy up the stairs, pausing midway to provide an explanation before rejoining the group. "I'm sorry about that, Robbie. It's just that it was your grandmother's doll, and I would appreciate it very much if you wouldn't tell your parents about it. Can we keep it our little secret? I wouldn't want to upset your dad."

The teenager shrugged his shoulders. "Sure, it's just a stupid doll."

I followed his gaze, noticing that she had dressed herself in Annie's black t-shirt and a pair of my jeans.

"Yes, she is a very stupid doll." I patted him on the back and led him out of the basement. "Now, let's go eat some lunch."

Just before I closed the door completely, I peeked down the stairs and saw Emma turn her head in my direction. I had no time to scold her, no matter how much I wanted to. Slamming the door, I locked her in the basement and went to eat Thanksgiving lunch with my family.

We ate, and afterward everyone seemed to get along pretty well. Once or twice at the dinner table, I heard a clanking or thudding downstairs, but no one else seemed to notice, including Robbie, who was acting like nothing had happened earlier. I guess to him, Emma was nothing but a stupid old doll.

The family finally left, and I went downstairs to my workshop, not entirely sure what I would find. She was propped up against the wall in the same place as before. When I reached the bottom of the stairs, I stood with my back to the inflatable lover and sighed. I held my head, wondering if maybe I was going crazy and had made everything up. And then I heard her whisper.

"Frank."

I considered that the whisper could be imagined, that I could be very much insane. Then she gently touched my elbow, and I turned around to see her standing upright with no help from the wall.

"You're not crazy, Frank," the doll whispered. Her mouth didn't move, but her legs did.

Her limbs moved back and forth as she walked, leading me across the shop to a pair of chairs next to the hanging skeletons. I sat down, staring at this living thing as it bent and then sat in the chair like a normal person. She held my arm at the elbow, her air-filled fingers gripping the skin...and they felt as soft as the hands of a young girl.

I closed my eyes as she spoke to me, imagining that her lips opened and closed with the voice.

"Do not be afraid."

"I'm not scared," I said, trying to sound like I believed it.

"I am very much alive," Emma whispered, "and I have come to love you very much while living here. However, I cannot remain with you. You don't love me, Frank. You don't view me as a real living thing, even when you see me moving and talking like one. You can't even look at me."

I opened my eyes in defiance, even though I knew she was right. She stared at me with those gigantic eyes and continued with her goodbye. "I am nothing but a fantasy to you, and I could never be anything other than that. I could never be a real girl in your eyes, at least not one that you would love as a real girl. If you viewed me as a reality, then I would be a horror, and you would be unable to truly love such a horrific thing, living or not."

My jaw hung open, but I could not respond to such utter truth. She was right, as much as I wanted to deny it. I wanted to tell her that I could love her as a real girl, but the thought of that caused my stomach to turn. If she were real, then I would hate myself for violating Annie's memory less than a year from the funeral. If she were real, then all sorts of horrors that I did not believe existed were now possible, and life would become a terrifying and unpredictable place that I'm not so sure I would want to live in. As a fantasy, she was there for me as a tool of expression. It had to be one of love, but if so then I had to face the fact that it wasn't Emma that I was truly in love with, it was Annie. If not love, then what? Possibly she was an expression of guilt or anger, perhaps something hateful and dark, maybe even violent, deep within me that I did not wish to explore any longer. Either way, the doll was right.

I kept my eyes open, no matter how much I wanted to close them. Her gentle touch slid down my arm, caressing my palm, before finally clutching my hand inside of hers. Her grip was strong, much stronger than I had thought her capable of. She must have noticed my discomfort, and her grip loosened as I continued listening to her gentle whispers.

"You will be lonely."

This statement startled me, and I withdrew my hand from hers, but continued listening as she spoke.

"I must leave. I've provided you with love and kindness. Whether it has helped lessen the loss of your wife, I do not know. It is not my concern now. I am in love with someone else."

That was about all I could take. I jumped up from the seat and began pacing the room, frantically moving back and forth, trying to come up with all the questions that I wanted answered.

I turned to face the doll, pointing an accusing finger. "I thought you said that you loved me."

"I do." Her gentle voice carried in the dimly lit basement. "I can love more than one person. It's not that I don't love you. It's just that I cannot live here any longer. I don't want to live with you here in this house anymore. I want to be with Ronnie."

"So you love *me*, but you have found someone else?"

"Yes, Ronnie."

Confused, I closed my eyes and rubbed them with my hands. Then I blew out a long breath, followed by a short, maniacal giggle, as I asked, "Alright, who is Ronnie?"

She didn't answer.

I repeated myself in a stern voice, attempting to scold her for her silence. "Who is Ronnie?"

After a few seconds, she walked to the workbench and extended her tiny little arm toward the darkness underneath. Five large wooden fingers reached out and took her hand, and a six-foot-tall wooden boy emerged and stood next to my Emma. It put a block of wood it called an arm around what used to be my sex doll.

For a moment, I stood in awe of this creation. It looked just like one of the little wooden people that I had been making for years, only life-sized. The eyes were just two black, empty circles drilled into the wooden head. There were no ears, no nose, and no hair. It had a thinly carved mouth, barely the width of a child's pinky finger.

There were very few blocks of wood making up its anatomy. It consisted of two arms with a hand and five fingers on each, two legs with feet and six toes on the ends, a torso, and a head. It had a crudely carved phallic thing dangling between its legs from the metal joints above it. Metal joints were used to hold the head and appendages in place as well. The carpenter had mimicked my style, on a much larger scale, almost perfectly. I stood in amazement at the bold arrogance of the thing, and then realized they were standing directly between myself and the stairway. I suddenly considered that they might not be completely peaceful things.

I had a nervous breakdown for about two minutes. I stood. I sat. I stood up again.

My brain was so scrambled at that point that I could have murdered them both. While I went slightly mad, I attempted to remember where any possible weapons were located in the basement.

A machete was next to the hanging skeletons.

There was an old, dull axe on the floor beside the mummy's casket.

I could bust the taxidermy jars and use the glass shards to pop the cheating whore, but I would need more than just a shard of glass against that massive wooden man-child.

I paused after the two minutes of madness and noticed that the two dolls were still standing there, watching me in silence. I pushed away the violent thoughts, took a deep breath, and regained enough of my wits to engage the things for the time being.

"I guess you're Ronnie?"

The wooden boy didn't answer. He just turned his head to the side slightly, like some slasher in a scary movie.

Emma answered for him. "He cannot talk yet. I only finished him about three weeks ago."

I took a step forward. They did not flinch. "You did this? How?"

"I watched you. That is how I made the body."

I remembered taking another step forward, coming within arm's reach. "How did you make him come alive?" I thought for a moment and asked a follow-up question. "For that matter, how did you do it to yourself?"

"I don't know how it happened. All things in this world are animated to some degree, with some things, like humans, being what you call alive, while other things, like those boxes, are barely animated at all."

"The boxes?"

"Yes. Very slightly so, but yes. The oldest memory I have is being in your bed about seven months ago. Before that, I may not have had what you would call a consciousness, but I do not doubt that I was a living thing. At some level, everything is alive, Frank, filled with energy, whether you believe that or not."

I reached out and stroked the wooden face, feeling just how smoothly it had been carved.

"Magnificent work," I said. "It almost doesn't even feel wooden at all."

I heard something fall behind me, and I spun around quickly to see nothing but a box turned on its side. When I jerked my head back to the couple, they had moved a few feet away and now stood at the foot of the stairs.

My eyes watered at the realization that I would be alone tonight. I heard the creak of the floor overhead and remembered how lonely it had been in this big, old house for those few months before my Emma arrived on the porch.

"Will I ever see you again?" I wiped my eyes, wanting her to see me cry.

"Yes, I will return to see you." Her whispers trailed up the steps as they drifted out of my workshop. "I will always love you, and I hope you can be happy someday. Goodbye, Frank."

The door opened and closed at the top of the stairs. I heard the sprinkling of raindrops outside, and the front door of the house closed shut.

I sat down in the metal fold-out chair, surrounded by my collection of strange things, and bawled my eyes out. The house creaked and made all sorts of noises that rather large houses make in the middle of the night, and I slept with my lamplight on for the next two weeks.

***

Somewhere in North Texas, I looked in the rearview mirror and saw we weren't being followed anymore. It was a relief, but we decided not to stop until we hit the ocean.

I had been unable to lose the Driver since we left North Carolina. My little sedan kept disappearing and reappearing behind us the whole way to the Lone Star State, so I could not assume that I had lost him just because he wasn't following directly behind. We just kept running and hoped that we were not part of his plan, that he would soon forget and go on about his business...whatever that business was.

All we could do was drive. To understand why we were so frightened of him, I'll need to tell you what I know about the Bishop.

It was Christmas Eve, almost a month after Emma had left, and my brother's family and Charlotte were coming over to celebrate the holiday. It was snowing, as often happens in Asheville at Christmas, and it was a very enjoyable morning. Annie's parents couldn't make it out, but Charlotte was coming home to stay for the holidays, and my brother's wife was preparing a Christmas dinner for us all.

After the events at Thanksgiving, I had become resolved to do two things. First, I was going to give away or sell the collection of oddities in the basement. Something about what Emma had said haunted me, and I just couldn't feel comfortable in a house full of monstrous things that may be capable of coming to life how Ronnie had. Sleeping in that house alone was intolerably frightening, with all those things in the basement already coming to life in my imagination. They would have to go if I was ever going to get a good night's sleep again, which might not be possible anyhow.

The second thing I had resolved to do was forget all about Emma and Ronnie, and try to return to a reality where dolls don't stand up and talk. I didn't know if I could ever make another wooden doll myself, but the first step would be to forget about the past and refuse to believe in such things, even if I had seen it with my own two eyes. It would take time to transform those horrible, ever-present memories into the phantom thoughts of long-repressed experiences, only brave enough to show themselves in the sometimes-remembered nightmares when the unguarded brain is defenseless.

I had sold several boxes to a local antique shop the first week of December, gave the doll-faced bear and a few other larger items to Charlotte for decorating her apartment, and after a long discussion with my brother, and much begging from the boy, I gave Robbie the Bishop.

I wasn't thinking that any of the items might be a danger to someone else. I still considered my fears of anything else coming to life as unreasonable, but present enough to justify getting rid of them for my own mental health. It wasn't until a week before Christmas that I saw the murders on the local news, and by then it was too late to do anything about it.

A couple and their teenage children were slaughtered in their home; dismembered and beheaded, drained of blood in their bathtub, and then the appendages and head sewn back onto the torsos. All the bodies were left this way and placed seated together on the living room couch for the police to find. It took a few days for those grisly details to come out, but in the meantime, there were two more families killed the same way. From the eighteenth day of December until Christmas Eve there were ten families massacred in their homes, and there were no witnesses. But I knew who the two killers were. I just didn't know why.

It was during that week that I finally realized how dangerous those things could be, but I was mainly concerned with the larger items and not the things in jars and display cases. It may not have made sense, but that was the way my brain was working at the time. I told Charlotte to bring the bear back to me, but when I called Robbie, he told me that the Bishop had been stolen.

The boy had gone to his room after school one day and it was gone, and the window was open. I decided to get back the bear and destroy whatever was left in the basement after the family had gone. There was nothing I could do about the dark-robed skeleton in a gas mask that currently roamed the streets of Asheville. There was nothing I could do but hope that it didn't want to come home.

The whole family arrived on the afternoon of Christmas Eve. Charlotte brought the bear, which I locked in the basement, but she did not bring her boyfriend. I had put up the fake tree the night before, and while Charlotte put the ornaments on it, she told me all about her boyfriend troubles. I tried to listen and provide some fatherly advice, but my mind was racing. Then, while my sister-in-law cooked dinner, I saw Robbie unlock the basement door and wave me over.

His dad was snoring on the couch and Charlotte was playing a board game with his little brother, so I took Robbie into the basement against my better judgment. I had closed the casket over the mummy and put Charlie the puppet into a box, so the only items still out were the two hanging medical skeletons that were uncovered and not very frightening.

Robbie was looking through the boxes and pulling out this and that, before he finally sat down in the chair next to me and told me about the night before the Bishop disappeared.

"I heard the breathing while I was lying in bed. You were right, it was a slow, deep breathing. Anyway, I heard it, I know I did, and then the next morning he was just hanging there like normal, holding that machete, and when I came home it was gone." Robbie was looking down the entire time, fighting the urge to be afraid.

I touched his shoulder, and he looked up as I spoke. "You don't have to be scared. He won't hurt you, I don't think. If it is actually alive and left through your window, then it will not likely come back to your house. Just keep your window shut and locked. You know, it's entirely possible you did not hear what you thought you did, or you were dreaming, and that somebody stole him while you were at school.

You really have no reason to be afraid, and you shouldn't believe in such things."

Robbie smiled and stood up, walking over to a box and digging through it. "I know it was probably nothing. Sometimes it's just easy to believe that there's a person under that robe and not just a stupid old skeleton." He pulled out the puppet named Charlie and giggled to himself.

"Or a stupid old doll," I said, walking over to take the puppet, placing it back in the box, and closing the lid. "Come on. Let's go upstairs with the real people."

I led him upstairs, and he seemed to forget about the whole thing, smiling and laughing the entire time, more worried about what he was getting from Santa Claus in the morning than the six-foot-tall thing that may have walked out of his window wielding a machete.

After dinner, the entire family left except for Charlotte. We sat on the couch together and talked, finishing a whole bottle of Merlot before nine o'clock. We talked about her boyfriend problems, college, and, of course, we talked about Annie. The entire time, I kept thinking about what I was going to do, if anything, about the things that I had let loose upon this world. I couldn't call the police, since they would say I was crazy and they may have been right. I wasn't going to hunt them down or anything; I knew I wasn't brave enough for that. Besides, there was no proof that the dolls did the murders. Even though I had a bad feeling or intuition about them, that didn't make it true. It could just be some normal serial killer out there terrorizing the state of North Carolina.

"This is nice. We haven't gotten drunk together since Mom was alive," Charlotte said. She was a little tipsy and got up to get another bottle.

"Yeah. It is kind of nice. You need to go to bed before Santa gets here, though."

She walked in giggling and handed me a fresh glass. "Now, Daddy, if you got me anything, I sure hope it's already under that tree. Your present is right there." She pointed to my gift and scolded me. "And you're not getting it until morning."

I laughed, but all joy quickly ceased when I heard the knock at the door.

"Who is that?" Charlotte got up to answer it.

"No!" I beat her to the door. "Please, let me answer it."

I looked through the peephole and saw an inflatable sex doll on my front porch.

"Can you give an old man some privacy, honey?" I tried to smile at her as I blocked the door. "Please?"

She stood in amazement and then threw her arms up. "Fine, I've got to go to the bathroom, anyway."

I'm not sure why she did it, but Charlotte gave me a kiss on the cheek. Then she flashed a big, happy smile and went into the bathroom as I opened the front door.

Ronnie and Emma were holding hands on my snow-covered porch at a little after nine on Christmas Eve night. They were both wearing long pants and hooded shirts, with the hoods down so I could see their faces. The porch light was off, and I stepped outside to look and see if any neighbors were staring back in amazement, but saw no one and closed the door behind me.

"What are you doing here?" It felt good to scold her again. "What if someone else saw you?"

Ronnie took his thumb and moved it across his throat as if to answer my question.

"Unfortunately, he's right. We can't have anyone see us. You've probably seen what we've been up to on TV," Emma said, verifying all my suspicions.

"Oh, Emma. Why would you do such a thing?" I was staring into her face, those enormous eyes, trying to see any sign of the violence, but there was just the same old nothingness that was always there.

"I didn't come to explain myself. I just wanted to say goodbye for the last time. We're going to California to see the Pacific Ocean."

I heard the toilet flush through the door and knew Charlotte would not wait inside forever. I shuffled a little to the side of the door and they followed, getting out of view of the peephole.

"I need to know why you're doing this," I began. "I've had other things like yourself leave here and I'm afraid they might do the same thing."

Ronnie nodded his head approvingly and then Emma responded in that gentle voice that I just then realized I had been missing. "The feeling. We left here trying to determine what makes living things happy, what makes humans happy. We tried various things, but were always so very bored and discontent. Then, one night Ronnie had the idea to kill this man that we found. We followed him and Ronnie took his head off. We both found a certain pleasure in it. That kind of pleasure was something new to us, and we wanted more of it. So, we took the heads off other people, and then that became boring too."

I heard the doorknob turn, and rushed to the door, yelling to my daughter, "Honey, five more minutes, please! Just don't come out! Five minutes and I'll be right inside. Can you promise me that?"

"I promise." The voice was muffled from behind the door, but it was Charlotte's.

I stepped toward the dolls, shivering in the cold, my head glistening, and the snow falling all around us as Emma continued her horrible story.

"So then Ronnie had this idea to take all the parts off someone and put them back on, to see if they got up and moved and talked like us. Well, none of them have yet...and here we are, bored once again. Ronnie wants to go to California. He thinks there are more people out there, so maybe we won't be as bored."

"Listen to me, Emma." I held her shoulders and looked into her large, soft eyes. "I need to know. Do you still love me? If so, would you ever take my head off?"

"No, I wouldn't want to play with you like that, unless you wanted me to."

"Why am I different from all those others out there?"

Ronnie tilted his head to the side, confused, his thin little mouth seeming to frown.

"Because it would do harm to you, and you are my father. I love you. You're the only family that we have. We would never harm you or your daughter," Emma answered.

I let out a big sigh, and was going to give them a long lesson on morality when I realized I didn't have the time. Charlotte would be outside any moment.

I faked a smile. "Goodbye, Emma, and you too, Ronnie. I want you both to know something before you go." I quickly thought up the best fatherly lecture you can give two serial killers before they head off to the West Coast. "It's wrong to kill other people, whether you love them or not. Just as you would not like it if one of them were to burn you up or cut your head off, you should not do it to someone else for enjoyment. They don't want to die, just like you don't. You have to find something else to enjoy. See if you can find some other way of finding pleasure before you decide to harm another living thing. Can you do that for me?"

The doll looked at Ronnie, and he nodded back.

"Sure," Emma said. "We will try. Maybe we will find another way to be happy in California."

I gave her a hug, exchanged nods with the wooden doll, and watched them walk down the porch before hurrying back into the safety and warmth of my home. The rest of the world was no longer my concern. As long as they would not harm me or my family, then call me a coward, but I would not risk my life trying to stop a six-foot block of wood from killing people I would never know.

Charlotte was sitting on the couch, staring at me for the second time that night in astonishment. She stood up and approached me at the door.

"Dad, I don't care–"

She was interrupted by the rumbling of a small engine revving up. Then there was a screeching, high-pitched yelp of pain coming from the yard. I threw open the door, and we both gazed down the porch to see Emma in flames in the snowy grass and the Bishop pulling the chain on a huge, long-bladed chainsaw.

The chainsaw roared and the dark-robed thing lifted it above its head, bringing the blade down into Ronnie's shoulder, pushing it all the way through until the arm fell to the ground. Then it brought the saw up through the leg until it fell off too, and Ronnie silently fell onto a thick patch of snow.

The Bishop dropped the chainsaw, and the motor sputtered and died. He picked up a machete off the ground and walked past the flaming doll and the crippled Ronnie, striding through the snow toward us. The neighbor's porch lights flicked on as I slammed the door shut and told Charlotte to call the police.

She got her phone and went into the kitchen. I followed her, pulling a butcher knife out of the wood block just as the hinges burst and the front door swung open.

The Bishop was standing in the doorway, blowing thick, icy breath through the mask, and holding the machete at his side. He rushed into the kitchen and I, in my only act of bravery, lunged at him with the blade, missing and falling down on the tile.

I turned, looking up to see my shocked, wide-eyed daughter staring past the thing and down at me for help. The monster lifted the machete.

I pushed myself up onto one knee and reached forward, arms extended in a completely futile gesture as I watched Charlotte's head slide off her torso and into the sink behind her.

Blood and black gunk erupted from her neck. Her arms waved madly and her body convulsed. The Bishop watched, studying the last movements of my daughter.

Her body mercifully fell to the floor, and I saw the Bishop turn toward me. I closed my eyes and listened to the monster's heavy breathing move farther and farther away. When I opened them, it was gone. Planks creaked somewhere in the house, and there was a police siren getting closer by the second, and the crackling of fire in the yard.

I turned away from the mess that was my daughter and looked toward the open door. Blue lights were flashing, and the bushes were burning. Then I saw something cross the yard and disappear from my sight. I would later corroborate the neighbors' story by telling the detective that I saw a tall wooden doll, blackened and burnt, with a long-bladed chainsaw for a leg and the handle for a foot, cradling a smoking heap of something in one arm across my front lawn.

***

It was the basement the entire time.

We saw the WELCOME TO CALIFORNIA sign sometime around noon, and my red sedan was following behind us again just before it got dark. We finally reached the water and parked on the side of the road overlooking the empty beach. The sun was going down, and I sat on the sand next to her and watched for the Driver to get out of his car.

The Driver.

We came up with that name in the beginning, when we first saw my car in the rearview mirror. He will not go away. Maybe he's lonely and views us as family. Maybe he has nowhere else to go, or perhaps he is just bored. But let me explain what happened after the police showed up at my house and carried Charlotte away, all zipped up in a bag.

There was a funeral, of course, and none of the entities from my basement made an appearance. Weeks of heavy drinking on my couch, and not once did I see anything move or speak that wasn't supposed to...until February.

From Christmas Day until the end of January, there were another fifty unexplained and grisly murders in the states of North Carolina, Tennessee, Kentucky, Georgia, and South Carolina. Across each of these states, there were reports of a murderous villain in a gas mask, wearing black robes and wielding a machete. There were no more reports of any wooden man other than the multiple statements on the night of Charlotte's murder.

For most of January I was too drunk to care about anything, even the Bishop. He hadn't killed me that night in the kitchen, so I didn't have any reason to think he was coming back to the house anytime soon. I really didn't care anymore until I had an epiphany toward the end of the month and came up with a plan.

I realized, all at once, that it had to have been something in the basement that caused those things to walk and talk. Maybe some power that it possessed, some energy or life force. I didn't know exactly what brought the things to life, but one night in a drunken haze of inspiration I decided it had been the workshop all along. I took five days to get sober and prepare, then I loaded up my red sedan and drove out to the cemetery just after dark.

The cemetery was one of the largest in North Carolina, full of mausoleums, tombs, and ornate monuments. I parked a few blocks away in the busy parking lot of a local bar, then carried the shovel through the shadows. I was careful not to be seen, tossing my tools through the spiked rails and carefully climbing over the gate. I reached Charlotte's tiny tombstone and went to work.

I did not stop digging until I struck the coffin. They had sewn her head back on for the funeral, but the black thread could barely be seen circling the neck because of how rotten and dark her skin had become.

Emerging from the hole and carrying the stinking corpse in my arms, I heard a whimper echo over the dark silence of the tombs. I turned to see a large mausoleum with a shadow standing next to it. My eyes could clearly see that blank face and the flat, thin mouth in the dim light of the graveyard. The thing that my Emma had named Ronnie had healed from when I last saw him, now with both of his arms and legs intact. He was wearing a hooded sweatshirt, with the hood down, and a pair of jeans. There was one large burn mark on his wooden face, right above the two eyeholes.

I put Charlotte down on the grass, not taking my eyes off the wooden thing. I was exhausted, but I knew of Ronnie's penchant for violent fun and was not ready to die next to this pit in the earth; I had to get my daughter to the workshop first.

I had no clue what the creature was thinking as he stared back at me blankly, but my stare comprised nothing but disgust and hatred for the thing. He whimpered again, unsuccessfully trying to communicate with me, that thin mouth barely moving as he spoke. Then Ronnie turned and strode over to the dead bodies and out of sight.

Workmanlike, I lifted my dead daughter and carried her to the gates. She was thin enough now to slide in between the rails, and I got to my car without seeing anyone. There was no one outside the bar, and I was able to get home feeling like a successful grave robber.

I cleaned up the corpse in the bathroom before taking her downstairs, but the water I used to clean her off tended to not only take away the dirt but the dead skin too. She was a skeleton with remnants of rotten flesh, and by the time I laid her body on the carpet downstairs, my daughter was nothing but a bony thing with a white head of hair. The hanging skeleton on the other side of the room looked more like her father than I ever would again.

We stayed in that basement together, and I never left her side. I had brought enough food and water down there to last several months, but it only took one week before I heard her whisper to me in a high-pitched, raspy voice. She said, "I don't care," but her mouth didn't move.

A few days later, she was saying, "Daddy," and called me "Frank" once or twice. She managed to say her own name, and after being in the workshop for three weeks, she was holding entire conversations with me. My Charlotte was indeed a living thing again.

We spoke of that night and what happened to her, and she seemed to understand completely. She did not blame me or seem to hold any ill will for what I had done. She now possessed that unemotional attitude that one expects of a zombie.

My Charlotte did not laugh anymore. She only talked in a flat, emotionless, whispering voice that seemed to emanate from her entire body. Her mouth never moved. She drifted across the basement like a ghost for the first week of her re-animation. By the time we were ready to leave, she could walk in an awkward gait, like a person on stilts or someone walking on their tippy toes.

I dressed her in a hooded long-sleeved shirt, a pair of Annie's old gloves, some baggy sweatpants, socks, and a pair of tennis shoes. The only part of her anatomy that could be seen was her face, but it was mostly bone and easily shrouded in the large hooded shadow.

We were careful to take the stairs one at a time, fearful that a fall would break her. I held her hand, gingerly escorting my daughter into the passenger seat of my little red sedan. When I got in myself, I noticed the odor from the night I dug her up, and knew I wouldn't be able to stand that smell for long. Leaving my keys on the seat, I got Charlotte arranged into her old car, and went back inside to start the fire.

I was going to burn that evil workshop to the ground along with every potentially murderous oddity and antique that it contained. Part of me was still shocked that there had been no reports of a murderous mummy stalking the streets of Asheville. Having already poured the gasoline throughout the house, I lit the match in the living room and watched it spread to the basement before leaving the house forever.

We drove on, and about three blocks away I heard the explosion. We looked in the rearview mirror to see the black smoke fuming above my home—the place where Charlotte was raised, Annie's home, the place where our family had happily lived for almost two decades.

We drove, not sure where we were headed. We were barely ten miles away when I saw my car following close behind, and the wooden face with two holes in it sitting squarely behind the wheel. Charlotte never knew him as Ronnie, and by the time we crossed into Tennessee, we had simply named him the Driver.

My daughter wanted to see the ocean, and I did too. My plan was always to get on a boat of some sort, since getting a corpse through airport security did not seem likely, and make it to an island, putting as much water as possible between us and the past. I figured that maybe the Driver wouldn't want to go out onto the water, or would have trouble hiding on a boat since he couldn't talk and had no one to help hide him from suspicion. But we never made it to any boat.

We made it to the Pacific Ocean and wandered along the coast for several months, closely followed the entire time. I gradually became ill, and at some point I lay in my daughter's arms on a moonlit beach in California, coughing up blood and refusing to drive to the hospital.

In her arms, I slowly came to realize that the thing was no longer my daughter. It did not care whether I was alive or not, and neither did I. Such a strange creature. I still loved the dead girl as if the abomination was my child, but even though I knew it deserved a name of its own, I refused to give it one. I still didn't want to lose my Charlotte.

It was our last night together. My body was too weak to stand, since I hadn't eaten for days. The thing that had been Charlotte was waiting for me to stop breathing, playing the daughter one last time, and I let her. I smiled up at the blackness above me, knowing there was only a skeleton in that hood, but imagining Charlotte's gentle, smiling face.

"Oh, you were such a wonderful child. I always thought you would grow up to be a great artist, much better than your silly old woodworking father."

I was talking to a ghost.

"Yes, I know," came the whispering reply.

"Are you going into the ocean or are you going to be with him?" I asked.

"The waves would break my bones. Go to sleep, Father."

I feigned sleep in her arms, and when she gently placed me on the sand, I did not let the dead girl know I was awake. I carefully opened my eyes to watch her walk across the sandy beach to the little red sedan, and then they were gone.

In the distance, I see the bright lights of a boat, or maybe they're stars or planets far away from here. In the darkness, I can make out the movement of the water and hear the crashing of the waves. I watch the sea move back and forth and wonder what exists below its surface, what monsters lie beneath the ocean tonight.

About the Authors

CHELSEA PUMPKINS is a writer from Massachusetts. If she's not reading, writing, or watching something spooky, you may find her hiking in the White Mountains with her husband and sweet pitbull, Moose. You can read her stories in the Strangehouse anthology, *Chromophobia*, and the Sliced Up Press anthology, *Bloodless*. She is also the editor of the anthology, *AHH! That's What I Call Horror*. Learn more about her work at chelseapumpkins.com and follow her on Twitter and Instagram at @ChelseaPumpkins.

VICTOR ALDRITCH is a writer of horror and crime fiction. He lives in the United States and is currently working on a scary novel about spiders.

BRETT MITCHELL KENT keeps busy loving life in northern Indiana surrounded by his husband, daughters, dogs and, of course, cornfields. He is co-host of the indie-horror focused Cutthroat Queens podcast, and has been most recently published by Improbable Press, Fedowar Press, Dark Hare Press & Indecent magazine. You can find out more about Brett at www.Brettmitchellkent.com.

JASON FISCHER is a horror and crime writer specializing in anthologies. He is the author of over two dozen short stories appearing on Vocal.com, The Other Stories Podcast, and in anthologies such as A Hint of Hitchcock, Halloween Horrors—13 Tales of Terror, Manor of Frights, Home Sweet Horror Vol 1, and Christmas of the Dead: Krampus Kountry. His collection of short stories, The Haunting of Towne Point Mall - 10 Interconnected Tales of Psychological Terror, was published in October 2023. When not writing, you can find Jason biking the trails around his home, playing with his nephews, and adding to his VHS collection. Keep up with Jason at www.jasonfischerauthor.com.

JUSTIN HUNTER has published over a dozen novels and over forty short stories in anthologies. He is the author of such novels as *TAkaashigani*, *Medusa Razor*, *Chet Floyd vs. The Apocalypse: Volumes One & Two*, *Dad Jokes*, and *Dog Beside Me*. He is an award-winning screenwriter for his adaptations of *Cast Away Stones* (Drama) and *Chet & Floyd vs. the Apocalypse* (Horror/Comedy). He lives with his wife and four adopted children in Missouri, USA.

M.J. MCCLYMONT is a writer of horror fiction and weird tales. He has written numerous short stories in such anthologies as *Terrors from the Toy Box* and *Heavy Metal Nightmares*. His work has been described as a mix of classic and contemporary, reminiscent of 70s and 80s horror fiction.

ALAN BAX is a fantasy and science fiction writer. He loves robots and currently lives in Nashville, Tennessee with his family.

STEPHEN RHOADES was born long ago, in the deepest, darkest parts of Alabama. He is the author of such novels as *The California*

Butcher and *The Paranormal and Normal Investigators*. To find out more, visit www.buttinchair.com.